Gerald Hammond

Follow That Gun

MACMILLAN

First published 1997 by Macmillan

an imprint of Macmillan Publishers Ltd
25 Eccleston Place, London SW1W 9NF
and Basingstoke

Associated companies throughout the world

ISBN 0 333 68016 2

1 3 5 7 9 8 6 4 2

A CIP catalogue record for this book is available from the British Library

Phototypeset by Intype London Ltd
Printed by Mackays of Chatham PLC, Chatham, Kent

Chapter One

This story really began some time ago when, instead of being mother to a hyperactive but otherwise adorable child, I was only pregnant.

Traditionally, pregnancy is supposed to be a time for putting up the feet, indulging the taste buds and relaxing in preparation for the upheaval to come. Everybody kept telling me so and Ian, my husband, was considerate when he remembered. My father also paid lip-service to the theory but in practice went on just as usual, making demands on my time and energy. Dad has unblinkered vision in all other directions, but when he looks towards me a sort of mental myopia takes over. He knows perfectly well that I am a time-served engraver and competent at almost every aspect of gunsmithing; and he never hesitates to call for my help whenever he happens to need it, and yet he still thinks of me as about twelve years old. If not taken sternly to task he would reward me for my services with an occasional lollipop.

At the time, Dad also knew that in addition to preparing for the expected arrival and helping out in the shop whenever I was needed, I was trying to write up one of his earlier cases. (My friend Simon, a professional writer who usually undertakes this chore, was deep in another major novel and kept putting us off.)

Perhaps I should explain that Dad is Keith Calder, gunsmith and principal proprietor of the gun and fishing tackle emporium in Newton Lauder, a small town in the Scottish borders. But he is much more than the small shopkeeper suggested by those words – and this is not mere filial pride. He is for instance an occasional but successful inventor. He writes frequent articles of a technical nature, mostly about the early history of guns. He has built up the trading in antique weaponry into an important and very profitable side of the business.

And there is more yet. Nothing makes Dad froth at the mouth (metaphorically speaking) so much as when he is referred to as a 'private eye', but there is no denying that he has often been called in, usually by the defence but sometimes by the police, to assist in investigating cases in which firearms were involved, not always as weapons but just as often as valuable artefacts which have been stolen or falsified. Sometimes his technical knowledge and inherent nosiness has enabled him to suspect a crime long before anybody else has noticed anything amiss.

To return a little closer to the point, Dad phoned one morning to say that my help was required. I had more than enough to do at the time, what with the needs of my home, my husband and my forthcoming family. On the other hand, the day was fine and the flat was stuffy and if I dawdled there it was almost a certainty that Uncle Wal, Dad's partner, would phone and ask me to take over the even stuffier shop for an hour, a day or ever, whereas Dad still lived in the family home, Briesland House, a couple of miles outside the town, where there was air and space and a shaded garden. I said that I would be delighted to help but transport was required. Ian, my policeman husband, was away with the family car and I had no intention of trusting the next generation to the buffeting and germs of the local bus.

Mum fetched me in the jeep which is in theory her car but in fact acts as Dad's shooting vehicle. Mum makes do with whichever car happens not to suit him at the time. Mum is usually very accommodating but when she puts her foot down she puts it down hard. She dropped me at the front door, turned on the gravel and scooted away again to do some shopping and visit a sick friend. Mum is small and dark and I shan't feel that I have been short-changed if I look like her when I get older.

The house is Victorian, built at a time when space and quality counted, and is tucked away from unwelcome intrusion behind a tract of woodland on a byroad that goes on only to serve a small market garden. I was born and brought up in the house so that it is a part of my ongoing consciousness; but whenever I have been away, as now happens for most of the time, it comes as a shock to realize just how much more dignified and elegant and generally *nicer* it is than any other house for miles around.

I found Dad working in the garden. Not at gardening, which he gave up thankfully some years ago in favour of hiring the neighbour from the market garden. In fine weather, he transfers whatever he is doing into the open air if that is physically possible and, if not, he does something else until the weather deteriorates again. As he says, fine days are too precious to waste. He had run out an electric cable, set up several card tables on the grass in the walled garden outside the French windows and carried out a whole stack of electronic gear.

His first need, it seemed, was coffee. I made for both of us – a tarry brew for him and mild decaff for myself and the foetus. Preliminaries over, I answered a few searching but token questions about my state of health and we got down to business. I had to admit that it was not a task to be tackled single-handed. He had for years been getting by with the use of an outdated computer which had originally been designed as a teaching tool for six-year-olds. He was now transferring data to his new pride and joy, a state-of-the-art laptop with facilities that he had never dreamed of and would never fully explore. (I took my hat off to him anyway, because it must have been quite an undertaking to make the plunge into high-tech computers at an age when most men are switching off.) There was no possibility of an interface between the two systems so that any transfer had to be done the hard way.

The present task was the transfer of the list of antique guns held upstairs in the house. Dad's workshop and storage space had been squeezed out of the shop before I was born. At Briesland House, there is now a workshop with machinery for the larger jobs in the outbuildings, but for comfort and convenience Dad has a small work-bench in the space made by the throwing together of two large double bedrooms at the front of the first floor. Here, rack after rack held examples of the work of gunmakers of the past – brilliant, laborious productions of brown metal and glossy wood, patient engraving and refined mechanism.

It was not a job to be hurried. The list was prepared and adjusted regularly and with some care, because it was circulated to favoured customers at fairly regular intervals. But it was further complicated by the addition of certain symbols about which Dad was uncharacteristically secretive. I knew that the noughts-and-crosses symbol identified guns which were not part of the stock but were being offered for sale on behalf of clients. Others were held as investments on behalf of clients but figured in the circulated list 'to test the water' as Dad put it, in case the time had come for the investment to be realized. Again, some items which were ostensibly part of the business's stock were priced substantially above market value and marked with a symbol of their own. I was fairly sure that these were the guns which Dad regarded as his personal collection and that he had no intention of letting any of them go at any price. I had heard Wal complaining to Dad on the subject but without any real fervour. I think that he was only making the point in order to lend weight to some other argument. Even after twenty years, Uncle Wal is still grateful to Dad for taking him into partnership, and he profits very nicely from Dad's dealings in antique arms.

We worked away, not always in peaceful accord, for an hour or so. I read from a printout while Dad keyed the same data into the new machine. We would have got along more quickly if we had exchanged roles, but he said that he needed the practice and there was no arguing with that, so he fumbled and sweated and said words that Mum would have skinned him for if she had overheard him when he found that he had typed half a page in capitals. Dad was never a touch-typist. It was cool in the shade of the big sycamore where my swing had hung ten years earlier and all was quiet except for our voices and the monotonous calling of a collared dove.

We were beginning to think about lunch, but deferring any action because we were almost down to the end of the list, when we heard a crunching on the gravel of the drive and the muted engine sound of a moderately expensive car. The car itself was almost hidden from us by the shrubs that Dad and I had planted when I was in my early teens, but as it crossed the end of the path by the corner of the house we caught a glimpse. Dad must have recognized it more by the colour – a nice deep metallic blue – than by the shape, which was gone in an instant.

'Customer coming,' he said quickly. 'I'd forgotten that he was due today.' I heard a car door close. 'A good one. Don't contradict anything I tell him.' He raised his voice. 'This way,' he called. He put the printout away in its folder and turned down the brightness of his screen until it was illegible. 'You could fetch another chair,' he added to me. Apparently I was once again his teenage gopher.

I felt my eyebrows go up of their own accord. Dad, in his youth, had the reputation of being a complete rogue, according to Uncle Ron. (Ronnie is a real uncle, Mum's brother, not an honorary uncle like Wallace.) I had always found Dad to be scrupulously honest with clients. He had no scruples about diddling the taxman, and he and Wal enjoyed a sort of financial tug-of-war; but if he had reason to believe that somebody was doing him down he had been known to go to great and ingenious lengths for his revenge.

At first glance, I thought that the man who came

round the corner of the house did not look the type who would try to pull a fast one on Dad, until I reminded myself that a frank and open expression is the premier stock in trade of every conman. After that, his air of innocence began to seem contrived. He was small and slightly plump but very well groomed. In that summer's heat, not many men were retaining a jacket and tie and even the waistcoat of a suit of lightweight tweed, but he seemed not to be feeling the heat. His small shoes were sturdy enough for country wear but polished until they glowed. I wondered if his car was air-conditioned and, if so, whether he would give me my lift home.

I had fetched another garden chair from just inside the French windows and resumed my seat. Dad half rose to shake hands and sank back, gesturing to the empty chair. 'Have you met my daughter?' he asked. The man shook his head and waited politely. 'Deborah, this is Mr Foster. He acts for one or two major collectors – I don't know who they are.'

Mr Foster smiled, but I was watching his eyes and there was no warmth in them. His handshake was cool and dry. 'How do you do? Blooming, I can see. I'm very pleased to meet you. And your father won't find out what he wants to know from me,' he said.

'Quite right,' I told him and he smiled again. I saw his eye flick from my midriff to my left hand.

'I always enjoy coming here,' he said. 'You have, or had, a lovely home. Do you still live here?'

I explained that I was still a frequent visitor but that I now lived with my husband in the town. Dad, perhaps not wanting to seem too eager, had not offered the visitor any refreshment so I decided that it was not up to me to be hospitable in what was no longer my home.

That seemed to dispose of the preliminaries. Mr Foster got down to business. He produced a recent copy of the price list that we had been in the process of transferring and handed it to Dad. A number of items were ringed in red.

Dad was hiding a smile as he looked down the list. I watched closely. Just as I expected, Dad crossed off two of the most expensive items, a miquelet, breech-loading rifle by Franz Jeradtel of Vienna, dating from around 1650, and a pair of flintlock revolvers, beautifully engraved and chased, made by the Russian court gunmaker in the 1740s. 'These have been withdrawn,' he said.

Without comment, Mr Foster produced a red pen and ringed two more items. I noticed that he had again chosen from among the highly priced. 'If they're still available, I'll take these,' he said.

'Don't you want to see them?' I asked.

His look reflected my surprise. 'Your father has never let me down yet,' he said.

'We can do business,' Dad said. 'But the Danish nine-barrel snaphaunce has been in an auction and the wheel-lock pistol was written up in a magazine only a few months ago.'

'That leaves the two, then. The usual discount?'

'Certainly.' Dad handed me the list. 'Deborah, would you bring these two guns down?'

For the first time, Mr Foster showed emotion. 'Surely,' he said, 'your daughter shouldn't be carrying things up and down stairs. In her condition,' he added, as Dad looked blank.

To be fair, Dad was still seeing me as the schoolgirl who had always been around to fetch and carry for him. Now he blinked and shook his head. 'No,' he said. 'Quite right. I'll go up for them. Shortly.'

'Of course.' Mr Foster added up the figures in his head, applying whatever the usual discount might be, got up and walked away towards his car. He was back within two minutes, carrying a carrier bag which he handed to my father. 'Go ahead and count it,' he said. 'You won't hurt my feelings.'

For some obscure reason, I would have felt it rude to look fixedly at the bag of cash so I turned my eyes away. Dad's gunroom was in my mind, so I looked up at the window. It was open to suit the hot weather and I saw a starling land on the window sill.

'Keep still,' I whispered urgently.

Of course, they both looked up quickly. The sudden flash of two pink faces disturbed the bird and it took refuge in the room. Immediately, all hell broke loose. From two boxes high on the walls of the house strobe lights began to flash and there came a high yodelling sound that made me want to crawl down a hole and pull it in after me.

Dad got up and dashed into the house. The lights ceased. The din was cut off in mid-yodel.

'Bloody birds,' I said. 'If you'll pardon language unsuited to my delicate condition. They're a pest when it's as hot as this. I think they're looking for somewhere to nest. Either that or they're paying us back for netting the strawberries. It's the one unbreakable house rule

9

that the alarms in the gunroom are switched on whenever the room's empty.'

Mr Foster said something about sensible precautions.

Dad came out of the house, puffing slightly. 'I've phoned the Bentons and told them not to panic,' he said. He went back indoors, taking the bag with him. If this was a cash deal he would certainly count the money; and he had recently bought a machine for detecting forged banknotes. If the unusual Mr Foster was in the habit of making large purchases in cash, the acquisition might have been for his benefit.

I was left to entertain our visitor. It seemed pointless to mention the weather. 'Have you come far?' I asked instead.

For some reason, this idle query seemed to disconcert Mr Foster. 'It depends,' he said after a pause. 'Did you mean today?'

'I suppose I did,' I said. 'I was only wondering whether you'd stayed locally or had a long drive from home and this was your first port of call.'

'It's not my first port of call,' he said. After a moment he seemed to feel that a longer answer was called for. 'I'm on one of my regular buying trips. I have contacts with collectors and museums all over the world.'

'A nice life for a gun buff,' I suggested. 'Especially a bachelor one.' Still no reaction. 'Was your hotel comfortable?'

'Perfectly.' There was another pause until he again felt the need to gild the lily. 'I usually stay at the Newton Lauder Hotel.'

'They do you well there.'

'Yes. You know,' he said thoughtfully, 'your father

should get the alarms connected direct to the police station.'

He was quite right, of course. However, quite apart from the disinclination of the police to be troubled by starling-generated and other false alarms, there would have been little advantage unless the phone wires had been put underground and apart from the cost the only sensible route would have been over a considerable distance and through Belcast Woods where frequent forestry operations disturbed the ground.

But I was not going to tell Mr Foster that, although he had only to look up to see the overhead wires. I had to struggle to find something else to say. 'How long does your buying trip take you?'

He shrugged. 'Quite a while. It varies. It depends on how long it takes me to pick up . . . what I want.'

The conversation hiccuped again. But my interest had moved on from a struggle to make polite conversation to more positive curiosity. 'And you're away from home all that time,' I remarked. 'You do have a home?'

He smiled faintly. 'Yes,' he said, 'I have a home. I live abroad these days.' He paused. I raised my eyebrows and waited politely. No man can resist that gambit. 'Spain,' he said at last.

That seemed to be all that was on offer on that subject. I wished that Mum was present. When there is a world championship in extracting information without asking direct questions, her name will be the first on the trophy. Another part of my butterfly mind was wondering how he amused himself during the long evenings away from home.

'Do you shoot?' I asked him.

He shook his head emphatically. 'I tried it once or twice and didn't like it.' That sounded so much like the punchline of an old and rather rude joke which Ian, my husband, had once told me that I dropped the subject in a hurry.

I think that we were both relieved when Dad called to us from the front of the house. Mr Foster who, whatever my reservations about him, had beautiful manners, helped me to my feet and even offered his arm for the thirty-yard walk.

Mr Foster's car – dark, metallic blue, as I have said – turned out to be a huge Volvo estate, very suitable for the gathering of any antiques smaller than furniture. It was complete with every security device so far designed, which was only to be expected if he was in the habit of carrying large sums in cash. It took him some seconds to work his way past the various alarms and locks and open the rear door. The rear seats had been folded down to form a flat loadspace which already held several cartons; one flat box would have held a picture while others might have been full of books or china. There was no sign of cash but I noticed that a piece of rubber mat had been laid over part of the original carpet and I guessed that Mr Foster had had a metal box welded under the floor, similar to the gun-box beneath the floor of Dad's jeep.

Mr Foster's purchases – a pair of Brescian miquelets by Schiazzano and a German combined wheel lock and matchlock – were stowed, carefully padded with blankets. He shook both our hands, told me to take good care of myself and steered carefully down the drive to the by-road. A trace of fumes left hanging in the warm air confirmed the impression that I had drawn from the sound of the engine that it was a diesel.

Dad and I returned to finish our transcription.

When the last detail of the final tap-action boxlock had been safely transferred, it fell to me to prepare a snack lunch while Dad copied some of his more confidential material. My best guess was that this related to financial matters. Dad was usually the most open person in the world and I had no idea whether his uncharacteristic secretiveness was because he did not want us to know how rich he was becoming or that he was going broke.

I carried the tray out into the garden. The sun had come round and Dad had moved his tables away from the advancing sunshine. He put his printer down on the grass to make room for the tray. He told me later that the next few documents came out embellished with squashed ants but the printer was otherwise unaffected.

As we munched, I asked him, 'Are you going to give me a lift home? Or do I have to wait for Mum?'

'Of course I'll run you home,' he said indignantly and then spoiled it by adding, 'I'll have to go to the bank.'

'Mr Thomson will swallow his denture.'

Dad waved a slice of toast in a negative gesture. 'The bank staff are quite used to me making cash deposits. All the same, I'll feed it to them in drips and draps.'

'Should you be taking such sums in cash?' I asked him.

'On the whole I prefer it.'

'Are you diddling Wallace or the taxman? Or don't you trust Mr Foster any more than I do?'

In his agitation he choked on his last mouthful of toast and pâté and dropped an apple. 'Mr Foster is a *very* good client,' he said.

'But you don't trust him?'

'I never trust anybody in business dealing.' He looked round to make sure that Mr Foster was not lurking among the bushes. 'What are you getting at?'

'He doesn't add up right,' I said. 'Why does he deal in such large sums in cash?'

'So that he doesn't have to hang around while his cheques clear,' Dad said firmly.

'Don't you have to declare big cash deals?'

'In the States I would have to,' he admitted. 'Anything over ten thousand dollars. Here, the law's different. Cash transactions only have to be declared if there are grounds for suspicion.'

'And you don't think that there are?'

'No. What do you mean, he "doesn't add up"?'

'He's too polite – which, I may say, makes him a real freak among the men in my life. And I wouldn't have bought his Volvo second-hand. The model and the registration letter don't match. What's more, it's a diesel. Volvo didn't start putting out diesels until a year later. It's a ringer.'

'He could have bought it in good faith,' Dad pointed out. 'Since when have you been a car expert?'

'Since Ian started shopping around. For a policeman, he can be very gullible with his own money.'

'Anything else?'

'Mr Foster paid out nearly twenty thousand quid without even looking at the goods.'

'He trusts me,' Dad said, as though that were the most

natural and logical thing in the world. 'He's had a lot of very expensive goods from me over the years and he's found that his investment was safe. If he really has good outlets, he's made money.'

'He was evasive,' I said.

Dad looked alarmed. His hair, which is still thick and only slightly tinged with distinguished looking grey at the temples, seemed ready to stand on end. 'My God! You didn't put him through an inquisition?'

'Only to be sociable. Mum would have turned him inside out.'

'Your mother knows better than to antagonize a very good customer.'

That I thought, was probably true. Mum would have had Mr Foster's life history out of him and he would never have known that he had been asked any questions.

Chapter Two

After that day, I might well have forgotten Mr Foster, at least until he forced himself on my attention again.

For one thing among others, during that autumn I was delivered, as they say, of a baby boy – Bruce Walter Fellowes, it was later decided. It was a rewarding experience, uncomfortable but not so much so as to put me off the thought of repeating it. My own childhood was idyllic, but I had experienced the disadvantage of being an only child brought up in the country and although Ian and I – and Bruce Walter – were living in Newton Lauder, which was almost metropolitan by comparison, we had every intention of seeking rural peace as soon as this was financially possible. As far as I could bring myself to believe, of course, my own parents were immortal, but if the impossible should happen and they should ultimately cease to be around, Briesland House would come to me. At least one sibling for Bruce was definitely in the plan and, if nature should not prove so bountiful, travelling hopefully was almost as fulfilling as arrival and physically a great deal more enjoyable.

About Bruce, I could write a book – but this is not it. So I will only say that he had all the proper digits, put on weight at a frightening speed, hardly ever cried except when he was hungry or wet or windy and, because he cut two front teeth at a very early age, was very soon weaned.

On the face of it, life went on much as before; and yet the changes were profound. Being responsible for the well-being of two male persons who danced to different drumbeats. Seldom being alone except by prior arrangement. Exercising to get my figure back on the rare occasions when I was not doing anything else. Becoming known in a quite different range of shops. Even the pushing of a pram called for quite a different set of muscles from those used for merely walking.

Despite all my new responsibilities, Dad was never slow to call for my help, sometimes on the slenderest excuse. I soon realized that what he really wanted was to keep up acquaintance with his first male descendant, but once it had got through to him that I expected to be *paid*, and paid *well*, for every hour that I put in, and when he at last assimilated that his clients were as willing (if not eager) to pay for my services as for his, the money and the company were more than welcome. Soon, a duplicate set of baby foods, nappies and general paraphernalia was assembled at Briesland House. Sometimes, if Ian knew that he would not be home, Bruce and I stayed the night. But although we seemed to discuss every other subject under the sun, between Dad and myself Mr Foster's name never came up. It was quite by chance and in other company that his name, or rather his identity, was mentioned.

One damp morning in late October, I was engraving an expensive Italian gun for one of Dad's customers. (Italian engraving is generally very good but the basic

17

artwork is sometimes suspect. Their woodcock, in particular, tend to look like malformed storks. So the gun had been ordered with the lockplates left plain.) Dad had been outside, regulating the chokes of a Spanish sidelock, but had then dashed off in the family hatchback. The phone rang and it was Ian, for me. Sometimes when he found himself free for lunch when I was at Briesland House, he would invite himself to come and join us; this time, he suggested that I meet him at the hotel.

I borrowed the jeep. Mum insisted on keeping and feeding Bruce and I decided that I would be glad of a break, so I travelled alone along a road suddenly winter-bright now that the leaves had gone. There was a fresh chill in the air. I parked the jeep in the Square (which is more of a triangle), almost opposite Dad's shop. The public bar sounded busy but, as usual at that hour, the small cocktail lounge, a charmingly old-fashioned room of dark panelling and flock wallpaper, was empty.

Also as usual, Mrs Enterkin was in charge of the bar. Mrs Enterkin is the wife of the pre-eminent local solicitor and they are two of my favourite people. I am sure that she has no need to work, but she enjoys the company and, although she can be very discreet, she absorbs all the local gossip and scandal like a sponge. (Her husband says that she has to be squeezed like a sponge to part with it again.) She served me a tomato juice. I had gone right off alcohol during my pregnancy.

There was no sign of Ian. He was by then the Inspector in charge of CID in Newton Lauder and I knew that he was always subject to sudden demands from his masters in Edinburgh for a change to his plans. I decided to be patient.

Mrs Enterkin asked after the baby. I was trying to bring her up to date without becoming a bore on the subject when a man looked in through the glass door, failed to see whoever he was looking for and went away again.

'That wasn't Mr Foster, was it?' I asked.

'No, dear,' she said in her soft West Country accent. 'That was Mr McKillop from the plant hire firm at Craigie-knowe.'

'I thought not. There was a resemblance but he wasn't dapper enough for Mr Foster, I thought.'

She was puzzled, a rare event and one which put the only wrinkle in the perfect skin of her brow. 'The only Mr Foster I can think of works in the butcher's in Church Street and you couldn't call him dapper.'

'That isn't the one. I meant the Mr Foster who stays here sometimes. He was here about twelve weeks ago.'

'I can't think of any other Mr Foster, my dear,' she said. She took down another glass to polish. 'And I'd have known. I usually take over the desk while Maisie has something to eat.'

I felt myself frown and my natural curiosity began to stir. 'He said that he stayed here. He looked very like your Mr McKillop. He was less than my height, small but a little bit overweight.' There was no sign of recognition, so I went on. Small details kept coming back to me. 'Black hair carefully parted in a very straight line and slicked down. Small ears. Well-kept hands with a gold signet ring on the left little finger. When I saw him he was wearing a charcoal tweed suit along with black shoes, a pink striped shirt, white collar and a tie which I thought at first was a Watsonian but then I saw that it wasn't.'

'That could be any one of several, my dear,' she said. 'How very odd! Nobody like that stayed here. Don't look so worried,' she added cheerfully. 'Is it important?'

'I don't know,' I admitted. 'I hope not,' I added, because it had occurred to me that it would only be important if Dad was skating on thin ice. In the world of antiques, sharks are always swimming just below the ice.

She looked at me shrewdly for a moment. 'I shan't be long,' she said. 'Call me if anyone comes looking for a drink.'

She left me alone for about five minutes before she returned and, without seeming to think about it, resumed polishing another glass from force of habit. 'I looked through the register for June, July and August. Nobody named Foster. Nor anything like it, except for a Mr Forrester who was tall and grey-haired and only comes for the fishing.'

We looked at each other for several seconds. She seemed to be looking me in the eye a little too firmly. I had a sudden attack of intuition. 'All the same, you know who I'm talking about.'

She broke into a smile. She was more than 'a little bit overweight', but her skin was good and she had beautiful teeth. I thought that I would have killed to have a smile like that. But then, I would also have killed to be sure never to have to carry that much weight around. 'Not to be certain,' she said. 'Might he have had a dog with him?'

It was a measure of how much Mr Foster had perturbed me that I had developed such almost total recall about him. 'He might,' I said. 'He didn't when I met him, but there was a folded rug on his front passenger seat. It had white hairs on it.'

'Then they were in here for a drink,' she said, nodding. 'It would have been about then. Three months ago.'

'They?' I said. 'There's more than one of him?'

She leaned across the bar and lowered her voice. 'He was with a lady. One of the locals. I thought it was her dog at first, because she was making such a fuss of it, but later I saw him getting into his car in the Square and the dog was with him. A big brute of a car, black or dark blue, would that be right?'

'Spot on.'

She nodded again. 'I thought the dog was a collie,' she said. 'Then I thought a springer spaniel. It was probably a cross between the two.'

'And who was the lady?' I asked.

Mrs Enterkin looked at me in silence for a few seconds. I remembered her reluctance to spread scandal. 'I'm not sure I should tell you that,' she said at last.

'Why ever not?'

'He told you that he'd stayed here in the hotel. Why would he want to lie about that?'

'You mean, he stayed the night with her?' Now that it was pointed out to me, I could see that some of Mr Foster's evasiveness might have an explanation which, if not perfectly innocent, at least entailed no threat to Dad. But I was still uneasy about him.

'I may need to know more about Mr Foster,' I said. 'I don't think he's quite straight. It may turn out that he's pulling a fast one. Unless that happens, I won't breathe a word. But I'd like to be in a position to follow him up.'

'You won't say that you got it from me?' she asked anxiously. She was proud of her reputation for discretion.

'No chance!'

She studied me again and then made up her mind. She had known me all my life. 'It was Emily Shaw. You know who I mean?'

I shook my head.

'She has the antique shop at Coleburn.'

I knew the shop. Coleburn is only a hamlet, but it is on the trunk road which bypasses Newton Lauder. The antique shop, in what looked like a converted smithy, was well placed for catching passing trade.

'Is there a Mr Shaw?' I asked.

'There was. Probably there still is, somewhere.'

'Ran off, did he?' I suggested. But she only smiled vaguely. The lunchtime drinkers began to trickle in and on their heels came Ian, very apologetic because one of the big wheels from Edinburgh had arrived suddenly, demanding local knowledge.

Ian had to bolt his lunch and hurry back to the big wheel. I dawdled over mine, but I had no further chance to tap into Mrs Enterkin's fund of local lore.

I walked out into unexpected sunshine. As I reached the jeep, I noticed that our shop was already open for the afternoon's business. Wallace and Janet were going into Edinburgh and Mum was in charge of Bruce, so I knew that Dad would have to be in the shop. If I called to see him I might very well be landed with shop duty for the rest of the afternoon. Anyway, the subject of Mr Foster was closed between us. And if I went back to Briesland House I would have to go back to work. It was too fine a day for suffering indoors yet too cold for working outdoors, and engraving is one of the jobs that require the work object to be firmly held in a vice. On the spur of the moment I passed the byroad, joined the main road and drove the few miles to Coleburn.

The antique shop had been converted by somebody with taste and who also knew how to attract visitors. There were half a dozen cars parked in front and rather more tourists milling around inside. The stock, I had to admit, was good – streets above the miscellaneous junk usual in such places. A young male assistant was fluttering around the browsers but the real boss was obviously a middle-aged woman with blonde hair which I thought was basically natural but with artificial assistance. I studied her covertly while appraising an original claymore. She was of lean and stringy build, looking even thinner after an hour spent with Mrs Enterkin's opulence, and she had a hawklike face and not a lot of bosom. Her dress was conventional and modest but with it she wore rather too much antique jewellery: my guess was that she used herself as a display dummy. She was doing most of the real selling and I could see that she knew her subject.

When the young assistant was busy but Mrs Shaw was free, I went to her with a rather good powder or shot flask, Sykes patent. Her price was a little on the stiff side, but Dad likes to have a ready supply of minor items, to encourage first-time muzzle-loading clients to dip a toe in the water, so to speak. While she made out a receipt, I said, 'Did Mr Foster leave this with you?'

She looked at me sharply, weighing me up. Either she knew Mr Foster's name or else the flask had come to her through somebody who was not a faceless client. I could have known Mr Foster's name through the trade and have been unaware of any more personal connection with her. She shook her head and a moment later she was telling a Yorkshire family all about Spode.

Whether or not there was something nefarious about Mr Foster, no ominous rumblings came back to us. Frankly, I cared very little what dirt he might be kicking up, as long as none of it stuck to Dad. Life was full enough without inventing calamities.

So Mr Foster slipped out of my mind again and might have stayed there but for another encounter with Mrs Shaw.

The small shoot that Dad shared with Wallace and Uncle Ron was a fun affair and I managed to have my share of the fun despite the addition to the family. I was excused beating duties when Bruce was slung on my back, but Mum and I shared nursing duty and took turns beating or shooting and Bruce seemed to enjoy all the activity.

The shoot was intended partly for entertaining clients and business contacts (and Wal always managed to offset a substantial portion of the costs before tax). But a number of those contacts did not shoot live game, and so Dad, aided by the family plus Janet and Wal, always laid on a party each December. This had, over the years, taken on a form of its own, varying only to suit the weather. There was always a running buffet indoors with, weather permitting, an outdoor barbecue. For those who enjoyed it there was also clay pigeon shooting. As many traps were used as trappers and scorers could be conscripted to man them, throwing the clays from the garden across an adjacent field (by arrangement with the farmer, who was one of the keenest participants), thus permitting introductory lessons for ladies and younger shots and informal competition between the more advanced, for prizes which were valued by the winners far above their actual cost.

That year, the weather was kind. Out of the cold and drizzle came a day of frost combined with gentle sunshine. There was what looked like a full turnout – suppliers, customers, fellow dealers, one or two specialist outworkers, a friendly journalist and two policemen, colleagues of Ian, who had been invited along because it never does any harm to keep on the right side of the fuzz. For once Mum, who had spearheaded the culinary preparations, had no need to be too worried about her carpets because much of the food was being taken out of doors.

Dad, as usual, was busy doing the social thing. Uncle Ronnie was in charge of the barbecue while Mum looked after the rest of the food and Janet tended the bar. Wal and I were taking turns in giving instruction to the novices and, between times, nosing around to see what else might need doing.

I had just handed over the beginners to Uncle Wal when I met Mrs Enterkin coming away from the direction of the competitive traps. Mr Enterkin, being the firm's solicitor, was always invited and greatly enjoyed the food and drink. He was a wholly urban animal, did not shoot and considered that the only justification for the existence of farmland was the amount of litigation generated by it. Yet he had married a farmer's widow who was a very competent shot; indeed, she had just completed the course with a score that many of the men would have given their eye-teeth for. I recognized the twelve-bore over her arm – I had cut away the toe of the stock for her, to prevent any conflict with her imposing bosom. She had offered to take over the bar from Janet but had been firmly told to go and enjoy herself.

We were chatting – absently, in my case, while I looked around to satisfy myself that all was going well and the guests were enjoying themselves – when I saw her glance over my shoulder. She looked amused for a moment and then excused herself and went in search of her husband or a comfortable seat, possibly both.

I looked where I thought that she had been looking but without at first seeing anyone or anything significant. Guests were clustered around the barbecue. The hardier souls were circulating on the lawn instead of retreating into the house and hogging the fires. I looked again. Mrs Shaw was very competently managing a plateful of barbecued venison and salad and a glass of wine while talking to a man who looked vaguely familiar. When I mentally removed his skeet vest and dressed him instead in a dark business suit, I recognized him as James Hart-hill, pillar of one of the auction houses, to whom we were indebted for the occasional tip-off when something special in the way of firearms was coming under the hammer.

Mr Harthill collected a bagged gun from a nearby seat and headed in the direction of the clay pigeons. Mrs Shaw turned towards the French windows. I managed to place myself where she would have to notice me or tread me flat.

'Hello there!' I said.

She looked at me for a second or two before she said, 'Hello. You were in my shop not long ago. You bought something.'

'A flask,' I said. She looked doubtful. The word probably had quite a different connotation for her. 'Brass,' I added. 'Sykes patent. Powder or shot for the dispensing of.'

Her supercilious expression might have been habitual or a freak of physiognomy but it certainly intensified. 'Powder *or* shot? Couldn't you tell?'

'There's no difference,' I explained. I may have allowed my tone to become as patronizing as hers had been. 'The volume of the gunpowder and of the shot for a given black-powder load was similar.'

'I didn't know that,' she admitted. I respected her, very slightly, for being honest when many others would have tried to bluff it out.

'I wondered who it had come to you from,' I said. 'I did suggest Mr Foster, but you said not.'

'I don't think I know your Mr Foster,' she said, looking genuinely blank.

'I thought that I saw you with him during the summer. You were having a drink in the hotel.' She still looked blank. 'About my height or a little less. Dark. Well groomed and quite remarkably polite.'

The last word did it. I saw the penny drop. She glanced round, apparently to be sure that James Harthill was out of earshot. 'If you mean who I think you mean,' she said, 'his name isn't Foster. We seem to have a case of mistaken identity here.' She shivered momentarily and rubbed her upper arms against her body. 'Do you mind if we talk inside? I'm not really dressed for the great outdoors.'

We went inside. She took off a thick camel coat and it was immediately clear why she had been feeling the cold. Her dress had certainly not been chosen for its warmth. I removed several layers of coats and continued down to the last sweater. I claimed drinks for both of us. Janet seemed to be queening it at the dining-room table, which was functioning as the bar.

Emily Shaw accepted the fresh drink and looked around the room.

'Did he bring you that powder flask?' I asked her.

'As a matter of fact, yes.'

'If his name isn't Foster, what name do you know him by?'

She looked around again but more covertly. There were other drinkers in the dining room but nobody was paying us any attention. 'I don't think we're talking about the same person,' she said, 'but, if we are, what business is it of yours?'

When it comes to answering a question with another question, I am as good as the next one. 'Why should you care whether I know his name or not?'

'Do we have to discuss it here?' she asked petulantly although the other drinkers were beginning to talk far too loudly to overhear us.

'Not necessarily.' I led her through into Dad's study, which was out of bounds to casual visitors. We settled in two of the leather armchairs. 'What did he call himself?' I asked again. On a guess, I added, 'I won't say a word to Mr Harthill.'

She looked so indignant that I knew that I was right.

Mrs Shaw had designs on James Harthill who, I recalled, had been subjected to a rather smelly divorce a few years previously. I thought that a marriage between the two businesses would make economic sense. Whether the two could make it as a couple they would have to find out for themselves – if Mrs Shaw succeeded in her designs, which seemed to be well on the cards. She struck me as a determined woman.

'He told me that his name was Edwards,' she told me reluctantly. 'Julian Edwards. I hardly knew him, except in the way of business.'

Mrs Enterkin's suspicion that she had also provided him with overnight accommodation – and, by implication, the hospitality of her bed – was not evidence. It was not even relevant, just mildly interesting. 'So he sold you that flask,' I said.

'That and a few other oddments. He was more of a buyer than a seller. Pictures mostly, but always small. He didn't seem to mind what he spent. I found him a sea-scape by E. W. Cook and I know that he paid thousands for a Luke Fildes painting. He usually only went for the most expensive goods and always in cash, but never anything with any kind of a history.'

'You mean, like having been in an auction catalogue or mentioned in an article?' I suggested.

'That sort of thing, yes. And yet I remember him buying a box of odds and ends, mostly thin leather straps and silver bells and a feather or two; and once he went off with a fake carriage lamp. I was surprised at him, descending to that sort of tat.'

Mr Foster, alias Julian Edwards, was sounding fishier and fishier. One may call oneself by any name that one fancies provided that there is no intention to defraud. But a dealer who makes his purchases by paying out large sums in cash needs to be seen to be above board, and going by more than one name is not a step in that direction. Why he should specialize in goods with no publicly recorded history, I could only guess.

'When do you expect to see him again?'

'I don't,' she snapped.

'Oh?'

After a pause she decided to continue with frankness. At least, I hoped that it was frankness and not invention. 'On his last visit, the time that you saw us in the hotel, he bought a snuffbox, Regency style. He paid the asking price but then came back a day later. He'd had it valued – would you believe? – or else he'd tried to re-sell it – and he'd been told that it was a Victorian copy. Well, I'd never warranted it as genuine and he should have known from the price that it was doubtful. Mind you, I was going off him anyway. The business is full of shady characters but he was a little bit too much. And I'd seen him speaking to Toby Douglas.'

'Who's Toby Douglas?'

She looked at me as though I had uttered a dirty word, although she had uttered it first. 'Dear me, you *are* young and innocent. Toby Douglas comes even further down the scale. You must know him,' she said. 'He's a rat-faced little man, middle-aged but wrinkled enough to pass for a hundred, bald as an egg. He brought me some silver once, rather damaged, part of a lot which had been thrown in with something more important. He admitted that he'd had your dad touch up the engraving.'

'That was my work,' I told her. 'But I never met the client.'

She looked at me for the first time as though I was a real person and seemed more ready to let her hair down; or else the fresh drink was getting to her. 'Is that so? Maybe we can do business again. Anyway, Toby Douglas is a dodgy little squirt on the outermost fringe of the antique trade. He works out of a store in Grangemouth or Falkirk or somewhere like that in the Central Belt. He tried to palm me off with a fake set of Martinware once. I told him to go and bowl his hoop but my assistant, who knows a bit more than is good for him, warned me not to antagonize the man because his angle in the business is definitely the rougher slant, collecting bad debts and paying off scores for others. Not that he goes in for the rough stuff himself, he's not built for it, but if you want somebody intimidated he can recruit the men you need.

'All the same, I can do without knowing anyone who knows that sort of person. It's too easy to get drawn into the shady stuff in this line of business. So I offered Toby Douglas a good enough deal on a Georgian silver teapot that he wouldn't want to mess with me until the deal was concluded—'

'And you took your time finalizing the deal?' I suggested.

'You've got it. Maybe you have a future in antiques after all. Then I told Julian, or Mr Foster or whatever we want to call him, that I'd sold the snuffbox in good faith and he shouldn't be in the business if he couldn't get it right or take the knocks. Those impeccable manners began to slip and the accent as well. He said that he only did business with people he could trust.' There was a spot of high colour in each of her cheeks which was not accounted for by the careful makeup. 'I said that he couldn't do a lot of business in the antique trade with that attitude and he said that I'd be surprised and I told him not to come back. He said that it would be a cold day in hell before he did.'

Mrs Shaw, I had decided, was a man-eater. I would have liked to ask her which of the two men was the better lover, just to see her reaction, but there were other questions which had priority. 'Was the dog his or yours?'

'His, unfortunately. He was a nice-natured tyke, too nice natured to belong to a heavy-handed master. I like dogs,' she added, as though confessing a weakness.

I refused to be diverted into dog-talk. 'Do you know where he lives?'

'I've no idea. Not even a phone number.'

It sounded very much as though Mr Foster had wanted to be untraceable. But people leave behind them more traces than they realize. 'You said that his accent began to slip,' I reminded her. 'When that happened, where would you say he came from? Where was he brought up?'

Mrs Shaw's own accent was neutral, typical of the educated local, but dealers soon learn to notice and evaluate the customer, and the accent is perhaps the first yardstick. Sure enough, she only had to think for a moment. 'Up north,' she said.

'Highland?'

'No, it didn't have the lilt. It was harsher, east rather than west. I'd say north-east, and not from a city. Somewhere between the Tay and the Moray Firth.'

'That embraces a wide range of local accents,' I
pointed out.

'Maybe. He didn't slip very much and I don't really
know accents north of the Forth–Clyde Valley,' she said,
sounding as parochial as a Londoner talking about Wat-
ford Gap. 'Why are you asking all these questions?'

'He's been buying antique guns from my father. He
didn't seem quite kosher.'

'He isn't,' she said simply. 'But his money's kosher.
Take it, that's my advice. After all, you're selling, not
buying.' She looked into her glass. 'I could use another
drink. And then I'd better go and find Jamie Harthill, if
he's finished trying to shoot those poor little black things.
They may be inanimate but they have my sympathy all
the same.'

'I dare you to go and stand behind him and cheer
whenever one of them escapes.'

She smiled grimly. 'You do it. Men don't have any
sense of humour when it comes to those macho activities.'

I led her back to the dining room and supplied her
with another drink. She carried it away in search of Mr
Harthill.

I did not manage to get Dad to myself until the party
was over and the clearing up finished, by which time
he was in rather too good a mood to discuss Mr Foster.
When I saw him again, two days later, I reported all that
I had learned.

At first his attitude echoed Mrs Shaw's: *If the money's
good, take it and laugh all the way to the bank.*

'He could be setting you up for the big sting,' I pointed
out. 'He won't touch goods which can easily be identified
again, remember. He could be preparing to launder the

money from a bank job, or to get into the gunroom, or threaten to accuse you of stealing the guns—'

As it turned out, one of my suggestions was not so very wide of the mark.

Dad interrupted me. 'All right,' he said irritably. 'Don't go on and on.' He was not so much annoyed by my persistence as saddened by the thought of giving up a valuable outlet. He sighed. 'You could be right. I'll knock his name off the distribution list and we'll have to make more use of the auction houses again and pay their commissions.'

'With a good chance of a better price,' I suggested.

'Better than Foster was prepared to pay? I have my doubts. About once in four, perhaps. I'd rather have spot cash and a fixed price than take my chance at auction, any day of the week. When something major doesn't fetch its price, the word goes round that there's something wrong with it.'

We left it there.

Chapter Three

Once again Mr Foster-Edwards was relegated to a spot somewhere at the back of our collective consciousness. If he showed his face again he would have some tricky questions to answer. That, at least, was my view, but I had a suspicion that if he wished to pay top whack for an expensive gun – and remember, there is no upper limit on the value of museum pieces – Dad would take the cash first and ask questions afterwards.

Without telling Dad, I did go so far as to ask Ian about Mr Foster-Edwards. Like the discreet police officer that he is, my husband made no comment; but he must have taken my doubts seriously and done a check by computer, because when he came home the next evening he told me that nobody of either of those names was known who bore any resemblance to my description nor, when fed that description, had the computer lit up and said 'Tilt', or whatever it is that the new electronic games say when surprised. It was a pity, Ian said, that nobody had thought to take a photograph or to preserve Mr Foster-Edwards's fingerprints, which, as I told him, was easy to see in hindsight.

When his identity, or what passed for an identity, next surfaced, we had just emerged from one of the coldest, wettest springs in living memory. Then, as it seemed overnight, the temperature had leaped up, the rain had ceased, the wind had dropped and a gentle sunshine cosseted the land. Buds popped open, birds sang and young men looked at girls as if knowing which summer dresses hid lacy underwear.

My life was less glamorous, but then I had already fulfilled my reproductive function for the first time. I was struggling with the duties of a wife, mother and housekeeper when Dad phoned. My first thought on hearing his voice was that he was going to demand my services as usual to help him at the workbench, take over the shop or do a round of the snares on the family shoot, thus giving him and Mum a clear run with their first and only grandchild. I would have been a willing conscript. The flat was claustrophobic, the great world outside was calling and babies may be beautiful but enough is enough.

For once I was wrong. True, Dad demanded my presence as a matter of great urgency; but he made it clear that Ian was in as much or even more demand. Bruce was not even mentioned. I got on the phone, cajoled my way past an over-protective sergeant and spoke to Ian.

Ian, as it happened, was free or could free himself. I called Dad back to tell him so. Ian collected Bruce and me and drove slowly out of the town. He always drove with extra care when Bruce was with us and I could not make up my mind whether to be pleased or insulted.

Briesland House was looking its best but we were not allowed time to admire the show of bulbs and rock plants. Dad whisked us inside and Mum took Bruce off my hands. She seemed to be as puzzled as we were.

Dad's study was still his pride and joy. For half his

life he had hankered for a book-lined room, panelled and furnished with genuine antiques or accurate facsimiles; and when he had attained it, it never palled. That day, however, its atmosphere did not have its soothing effect. Dad was definitely in overdrive. He pointed vaguely to the spare chairs and then to the visitor, a man who was just getting up. Dad muttered a name.

Ian, who was nicely brought up, shook the stranger's hand. 'I'm Inspector Fellowes,' he said. 'Ian, outside business hours. My father-in-law mentioned your name, but not loudly enough for me to catch it. And this is my wife, Deborah. Let's all sit down.'

I nodded and smiled. The stranger did the same. 'Kenneth Foggarty,' he said. He was small, lean and silver-haired, brisk like a terrier. His clothes had never been expensive but they were clean and he was well shaved with a tidy haircut. He had pride in himself, I decided, but either he was short of readies or he was in a trade in which good clothes were easily spoiled or else, perhaps, he believed that an impecunious appearance was a help towards driving a hard bargain.

Dad had dropped into the swivel chair behind the desk. There was a gun on the desk but I had not paid it much attention. There was usually a gun on the desk, so that the leather insert had gradually become stained with gun-oil.

'I've done a lot of business with Ken Foggarty over the years,' Dad said, by way of finishing the introductions. 'He doesn't have a shop but he buys and sells a lot of antique weapons from an Edinburgh lockup.'

'I know the name,' I said.

Ken Foggarty nodded briskly. 'I represent a syndicate

of businessmen. They treat the guns as an investment – and a very difficult one to tax,' he added with a smile. From his accent I could have picked him out as genteel Edinburgh from a crowd of Scotsmen. 'Very often under-valued, too. I buy on their behalf and sell – usually through your father – when the price seems right.'

'And today he brought me this,' Dad said. He picked up the gun. I saw that it was a double-barrel flintlock from the early nineteenth century, certainly French and probably by Boutet, very ornate with inlays of silver, gold and mother-of-pearl.

'It's very like one that you used to have,' I said.

'It's the same one. I'd have known it anywhere. I've drooled over those Zaoué locks often enough. And Ken was offering it to me for slightly less than Foster, or whatever his name is, paid me for it a couple of years ago.' Dad turned his attention to Ian. 'Did Deborah mention Mr Foster, alias Julian Edwards?'

'She did. She asked my advice. I couldn't find out anything about the man.' Ian rubbed his sandy head, his habit when puzzled. 'Is it so odd that the same gun should come round again?'

'It's damned unusual. Guns of this quality and value usually end up in museums, or in the hands of well-heeled collectors, and stay there. Of course, it's possible for a collector to run out of funds and have to cash in his assets. But in this case, there are some odd features.' Dad looked at Ken Foggarty.

'One of my contacts bought it at an auction in Phila-delphia,' Foggarty said. 'He sent it to me because there was a good chance that it would make more back in Europe, but I thought that it might be worth testing the market in Mr Calder's list first. I didn't know that it had already been through his hands. You see, the provenance makes no mention of him.'

Dad was holding a few pages of paper clipped together, very tatty and dog-eared. The provenance of any valuable object is only the accumulation of documents detailing its making and passage from owner to owner, perhaps with expert opinions and valuations obtained at any time of dubiety.

'The first two pages are genuine,' Dad said. 'The gun was made for the Comte Beaudout de Fayal and presented to the Duc de Nantes – in return for what favour is not recorded. From there on it's fiction – a fake but a good one. According to this, it stayed in the de Nantes family right through until the end of World War Two when it was bought by a British officer, one Colonel Henry Leonard White. The Colonel is alleged to have gifted it to his son, Leonard James White, some seven years before he, the Colonel, passed on – just in time to avoid death duties. It seems to have been Leonard James who sent it for auction, though why to Philadelphia God alone knows.'

'I could make a guess,' Ian said, startling me. Ian so rarely speaks when guns are under discussion that it was as surprising as if the gun itself had uttered the words.

'So could I,' I said. 'Several, in fact. Somewhere along the way it's been stolen. Or bought and not paid for. Or it's the subject of a dispute over ownership.'

Dad was shaking his head, but in the patronizing manner of one who does not want to discourage a child who is trying hard. If I had not been so interested, I would have walked out on him. 'Any item as important as this,' he said, 'the word goes round like lightning in the trade. I would have heard.'

'Sometimes,' said Ken Foggarty, 'the owner may not know that it's gone. If it was in a safe deposit, for instance, or if a really good fake was left in its place.'

'Time will probably tell,' Ian said slowly. 'In the meantime,' he added in the direction of Mr Foggarty, 'I suggest that you hold on to it. Your syndicate's title will probably turn out to be good, in which case they have a sound investment. But you don't want to risk prosecution for selling goods while having reason to believe that they may have been stolen.'

Ian's last few words were interrupted by the electronic beeping of the telephone. Dad, muttering an apology, put out a hand and picked it up absent-mindedly. I saw his attention sharpen in a rush. 'Mr Foster,' he said. 'It's good to hear from you.' He flipped the switch on the small loudspeaker linked to the study phone, most often used so that the purchaser of an antique can listen in while Dad discusses its history with a previous owner or a fellow expert. An electronics whizz-kid had worked on it for most of a day to make sure that no change of tone was detectable at the other end when it was in use.

Mr Foster's voice came through clearly, courteous as ever. 'Mr Calder, it's good to hear your voice too. Life is treating you well, I hope?'

'Adequately.' Ian was making every negative signal possible in human body language. Dad nodded and looked away.

'That's very good. I wanted a quick word with you.' Accents often sound stronger over the telephone and, now that I knew to listen for it, I could discern a trace of the accent that Mrs Shaw had mentioned. 'Do you remember the Boutet flintlock that I bought from you?'

'I think so,' Dad said. He winked at us. 'Nothing wrong with the provenance, was there?'

Ian blanched.

'Good heavens, no!' Mr Foster sounded shocked, as though such things could never happen between gentlemen. 'But I'm afraid that there's trouble of a different sort. It was bought by a wealthy collector as the centrepiece of his collection. Now his scapegrace son has made off with it, and with the papers. There's no doubt that he will be trying to find a buyer. The father, naturally, wants to recover it with the least possible fuss. So I'm passing the word around. If it should be offered to you, I suggest that you try to keep it in your hands, perhaps on the promise of finding a buyer, and let me know. Remember, the provenance will certainly have been tampered with.'

'I see,' Dad said thoughtfully. 'And how do I contact you? I only have a box number in Glasgow.'

'I'll be moving around. Call my mobile number.' Mr Foster quoted a succession of ten digits which Dad noted down. 'The owner is offering a substantial reward.'

'I look forward to claiming it,' Dad said.

Mr Foster chuckled. 'I look forward to transmitting it to you,' he said.

Dad was smitten by a sudden inspiration. 'By the way, which country was it stolen in? The laws regarding the ownership of stolen property vary.'

After a pause for thought, Ian held up an approving thumb.

There was a telling silence. 'In Britain,' Mr Foster said at last. 'My regards to your charming daughter. Goodbye.'

'You see?' I said as soon as the connection was broken. 'Stolen!'

'I doubt it very much,' said Ian. 'It was a good story but it didn't quite fit the facts. For one thing, he hadn't anticipated your father's very shrewd question. If he had really been trying to recover stolen property in Britain, he would at least have known that the English and Scottish legal systems differ radically. In England, and especially in London, under the doctrine of Market Overt, anyone buying stolen goods in good faith may acquire good title to them. In Scotland, that doesn't apply. "Britain" was no kind of answer at all.'

Ken Foggarty cleared his throat nervously. 'I take it that you have no intention of claiming the reward?'

Dad shook his head. I followed suit. 'Of course not,' I said.

Ian seemed to feel that a direct reply would be unnecessary and beneath the dignity of the police. 'Something devious and unpleasant is going on. Mr Foggarty, I assume that the purchase could be traced to you. I suggest that you keep a low profile for a while. And leave those papers with me.' Foggarty stirred anxiously. 'They'll be safe. And you couldn't make use of them just now,' Ian pointed out.

'I suppose that's so.' Ken Foggarty sighed deeply. 'I don't know what my syndicate members are going to say.'

'Don't tell them yet,' Dad suggested. 'I don't think the gun was ever stolen. The last section of the provenance papers is probably gone for ever, but we can probably recreate something which would pass muster.' He looked at me. 'You were right all along, Toots,' he said generously. 'Not about the gun being stolen. But about Mr Foster, alias Julian Edwards, alias anything else he cares to call himself, being a bad hat. I think that I knew it all along, but I didn't want to believe it of a superlative client. You don't find many like him in a single lifetime.'

Mum's birthday fell three days later. This was the one occasion in the year when she was not expected to do any catering. In previous years, we had usually taken a meal in the hotel, but now that I had a home of my own with the added problem of a young baby to chain me to it, there seemed to be a general assumption that I would do the necessary.

In fact, I had no objection, provided that Dad brought the wine. I get very bored with humdrum, daily cooking, but I always enjoy the challenge of a Special Occasion. I would normally have taken a duck out of the freezer, but Wallace and Janet were to join us and Uncle Wal had a heart condition and was watching his cholesterol, so I chose pheasant, which can be much less fatty if skinned instead of plucked. I thawed the last two from the freezer, roasted them the day before and sliced them cold. A good soup to start, strawberries and cream to follow and a finish in the grand manner with cheeseboard and port. Both cheese and cream were forbidden to Wal, but he never grudged others their pleasure and would usually go out for a stroll after the main course in the direction of the hotel where he enjoyed another drink, a chat and, we suspected, an equally forbidden cigar. Uncle Ronnie, who is stalker and ghillie to Sir Peter Hay, was up north on Sir Peter's business and so was to be the only absentee.

Ian was late home and barely had time before the guests arrived to shower and change out of the formal suit which he wore as 'plain clothes'. As I had pointed out to him, he would have been less conspicuous around the easygoing citizens of Newton Lauder wearing the slacks and sports shirt into which he changed, but in his old-fashioned mind he expected his superiors to equate informality with irresponsibility and dressed accordingly. Bruce had gone off to sleep like an angel and, between attending to his needs and putting the finishing touches to the room and meal, I had somehow managed to bathe, dress and tart myself up so that I was ready for the visitors when they arrived. The room, though lacking the space and dignity of Briesland House, looked well and I was proud of the table with its centre-piece of flowers.

Mum and Janet were partners with Dad and Wal in the business, so the strange events which seemed to follow Mr Foster around had already been discussed openly among us. Thus there was no need for explanations when, after a preliminary drink, we had taken our seats at table. Ian said, 'I have had some feedback about our friend Mr Foster-Edwards. Including four other names that he may possibly have used. Just which of any of them is original we still don't know. I have the benefit of a Videofit machine on loan and I'd like you both' – he glanced at Dad and myself – 'to come in and see what you can do. Come separately and then we'll combine them by computer. I'm asking Mrs Shaw to help.'

'Good idea,' I said. 'She's seen more of him than any

of us.' Only when I heard somebody make a faint sound of amusement did I realize that my choice of words had been unfortunate.

'So it wasn't anything as simple as theft,' Wal observed. He is thin, very intelligent, with the lean and hungry looks that sometimes go with brains. He is shy and intro-verted but a surprisingly good businessman. He acts as the firm's money-man and takes responsibility for the shop and for the angling side while Dad looks after guns and shooting. Mum and Janet both help out in the shop while I act as a sort of First Reserve to all departments.

'Nothing like as simple,' Ian agreed. 'Your friend seems to be part of a small team which has devised a new slant on money-laundering.'

'Drugs money?' Janet asked.

Ian shook his head. 'The drugs barons have their own laundering channels, tailored to their needs. This seems to be quite separate. There had been suspicions for several years that somebody had a way of making a large number of smaller sums of dirty money look squeaky clean. More recently, we developed a good theory as to how. But we had no idea who.'

'Who, then?' I asked.

Ian's soup had cooled enough to take. We waited. I was gathering the empty bowls when he resumed. 'We still don't know who, except for what you've been able to tell us. And Mrs Emily Shaw, of course. But at least we now know that it hasn't just been an amazing series of coincidences. A small but effective organization does exist.'

'Start with how,' Mum said. Dad was pouring wine but

she helped herself to tonic water. Birthday or no birthday, when the family went on the razzle she was the driver.

I was serving the pheasant from the hostess trolley that Uncle Ronnie, probably prodded by Mum, had given us as a wedding present, so I could follow what Ian said without difficulty.

'You do understand that this is in absolute confidence?'

We all agreed. And that was enough for Ian. He knows that we can keep genuine secrets to ourselves.

'How turned out to be very simple. It wasn't just the antique guns, they were a comparatively small part of it. They went in for holding a stock of small but valuable items with no public history. The kind of thing that might have been found in an attic or bequeathed by an uncle who didn't know its value. Say that somebody comes by money that wouldn't stand up to scrutiny. An MP who has asked the right questions or a civil servant who has steered the right permits through or someone guilty of insider dealing. Perhaps an official who has diverted arms around an embargo or a sportsman who has thrown away the match to order. Sadly, it goes on all the time. Call it bribery, corruption, sleaze or just plain fraud, whatever you like, the powers that be have started to look very hard at anyone in a position of responsibility who lives beyond his apparent means.

'Whoever it is, he – or she, let's not be sexist about this – usually won't want to leave the money mouldering offshore to await a retirement which may be years off. They want a Ferrari, a villa in Benidorm or a sex-change operation and they want it now. So they turn to Mr Foster's group, or whatever his real name is, and they come up with some useful item. "I need a new car," he tells his buddies. "I have my great-uncle's violin in the attic. Do you think it could be a Strad?" And, surprise surprise! – a Strad is what it turns out to be. For violin, substitute any other rarity that can be discovered unexpectedly or which just might have been bought out of a jumble sale.'

I had finished serving and resumed my seat. My mind was leaping ahead. 'Who,' I asked, 'is Leonard James White?'

Even Dad looked baffled for a moment but Ian immediately remembered the name in the false provenance of the Boutet gun, although he took his time before answering me. 'Just take it,' he said at last, 'that Mr White is a very senior Whitehall official who is being asked some very tricky questions and not, I'm told, making a very good job of answering them.'

'And I suppose,' Mum said, 'that all the dealers and auction houses are being warned against selling to Mr Foster?'

'And against handling anything with a questionable provenance,' Keith said.

'Of course,' said Ian. 'Locally, that's one of my jobs. Later, word will go round in all the areas where people may be subject to temptation that sudden discoveries of valuable antiques will be subject to searching inquiries. Until then, it may be illuminating to see who talks to who.'

Ian's revelations had opened up a whole host of topics to see us through the main course and the sweet. We had drunk Mum's health and were finishing off the cheese and biscuits when Wal, who had stayed after his usual time of departure to toy with a few strawberries and skimmed milk, said to Ian, 'There's one aspect of this that you're not telling us, isn't there?'

'I've been wondering how to open it up without spoiling a good party. How did you know?'

'It seemed to me,' Wal said slowly, 'that Mr Foster will have a pretty good idea as to who blew the whistle on him.'

Ian took on a solemn expression which was foreign to his usually cheerful countenance. 'I'm afraid so,' he agreed. 'And one of the few things we've been hearing about the gentleman and his colleagues is that when they're crossed they can turn ruthless. They have some effective underworld connections and they don't hesitate to use them. I've given orders that anything in the least suspicious seen in the vicinity of any one of us or our homes or property is to be reported immediately. It may be an unnecessary precaution, but I'm easier in my mind for having taken it.'

Several weeks slipped by. Wherever I turned there seemed to be a constable in view or a panda car vanishing round the corner. Mum experienced the same. She said that she felt like a goldfish.

When I said to Ian that Mr Foster seemed to have accepted defeat with his customary good manners, Ian looked doubtful. 'I'd like to think so,' he said, 'but that isn't the reputation of him or his friends. They don't usually touch stolen goods, because the business would soon have gone down the crapper, if you'll pardon my French, when the clients got caught up in that sort of trouble.

'We think we know who Foster is or was and if we're right he has a record as long as the street outside and with every force north of the Wash – under a variety of names, of course. It starts with car theft and burglary, goes on through confidence tricks and finishes with conspiracy to violence. The one time that somebody palmed Foster off with hot goods, we caught up with that somebody but he was much too scared to tell us anything useful. He already had lumps.'

'Then why have there been no repercussions?' I asked. Bruce was asleep at last and we were relaxing with a drink in front of the television. It was the butt-end of the year for programmes. There was nothing on but garbage. I used the remote to turn the sound off.

'If his usual contacts start telling him that they have nothing that would interest him, it might not dawn on him straight away that he is being given the runaround.'

'And when the penny drops?'

'Personal violence isn't his forte – he's too small for one thing. And when the word goes round that he's on the scrap heap, I'm hoping that nobody will want to know him any more. In his shoes, I'd gather up my savings and head for foreign parts, the more foreign the better.'

'Did you try to locate him through his mobile phone?' I asked.

'The company has been very helpful but he hasn't been making many calls, and those were from all over. None for the last week or so, which bears out the idea that he's gone abroad.'

'And his box number in Glasgow?'

'It's only a tobacconist's shop. As far as we know he hasn't been near it, but the shop was broken into a few

49

days ago. All the mail went, along with several thousand fags, so we can take it that he's caught up with his post and won't be going back.' Ian moved uncomfortably. I had been leaning back against him and his arm had gone to sleep. 'Anyway, don't worry about it,' he said. 'We're on the lookout and he's probably a long way away and much too busy setting up in some new line of business to bother with revenge.'

'I'm not worrying,' I said, fool that I was.

By almost unanimous consent, the following Sunday was a working day on the family shoot. A small wood, previously excluded from the lease, had suddenly become available. Dad and Uncle Ronnie had declared, first, that we must have it and, second, that birds must be released on it that same year. That year's pheasant poults were almost due for delivery, so the construction of a new small release pen was suddenly a matter of urgency.

The only person who would have been forgiven for being absent was Uncle Wal, who had damaged his heart by overexertion on a shoot working party several years earlier, but he pointed out that if ladies could be usefully employed on the lighter work then so could he. Even Bruce came along in a supervisory capacity. The only absentee, therefore, was Ian, who had urgent police business to attend to but promised to join us for the afternoon if he could.

Uncle Ronnie had prepared the ground the day before, hauling in the necessary posts and wire netting by Land Rover as far as the rock wall, higher than my head, which was as far as a vehicle could go. A narrow break in the rock held a short, steep path up which all supplies would have to be carried.

'If you'd put the pen down here,' I said as I got out of Dad's jeep, 'there would be a lot less carrying.'

Dad smiled and shook his head. 'If I was a pheasant,' he said, 'up there is where I'd want to be.'

The pen would begin about twenty feet back from the drop. Here the birds, six weeks old, would be confined until clipped wing feathers grew back and they could fly out in penny numbers, making their way back through fox-proof 'pop-holes' in the wire.

Uncle Ron had made a start to digging the shallow trench in which the foot of the wire would be buried to forestall burrowing foxes. Wal wanted to help Ronnie with the digging but Janet, who had at one time given an impression of coldheartedness, had shown her softer side when Wal became ill and sometimes seemed anxious to protect him from doing any work whatever. As a compromise, Wal was allowed to make post-holes with the 'podger'. Dad and I followed along setting the posts and Mum and Janet began to roll out the wire.

The day was pleasantly cool and misty, but the work was heating and the damp air brought out the midges. When, in mid-morning, we heard the sound of a vehicle coming cautiously up the ragged track, I think that we were each glad of the excuse to knock off for a few minutes, relax and have a drink and a chat. As we straightened our backs and sipped tea, the sun broke through. We had taken seats on hummocks of heather. To our right we could see some of the roofs of Newton Lauder peeping over a crest. Ahead, miles off, were the Cheviot Hills.

The vehicle turned out to be the Land Rover with

which Ian had been provided by a thoughtful Constabulary. He parked beside Dad's jeep and Ronnie's Land
Rover. As he climbed quickly up to us I saw that he had
not yet changed for work. Or at least, not for building
release pens.

Ian came to a halt near the middle of our small group,
towering over us. 'I don't want to make a stishie about
nothing,' he said. 'But I wanted to speak to you.' He paused
and looked doubtfully at my uncle, as well he might.
Ronnie, Mum's brother, is a rougher character and he
looks it. Dad once said that my uncle seemed to have
been carved from a log by a gorilla with a chainsaw. But
then, Dad and Uncle Ron have said many things about
each other, some of them true.

'I've told Ronnie about it,' Dad said quickly. 'He had
to know.'

Ian wasted no time debating the point. 'I asked to be
informed of anything unusual, however slight, in the
vicinity of any of us or our property. As it happened, I
was only about a mile from here when I got a message to
say that a car was parked in Belcast Woods, near Briesland
House. Empty. It's probably just picnickers or a courting
couple but it does no harm to be sure.' He looked down
at Dad. 'You told me that Mr Foster's car was a large
estate car, metallic blue. I suppose you can't be more
specific?'

'No,' Dad said. 'I'm damned if I can. It was a while
back, and at the time I thought Deborah was making a
fuss about nothing.'

'It was a Volvo,' I told Ian. 'A recent model. Diesel.
I don't remember the registration, which has probably

changed anyway, but the letters were Aberdeenshire and it dated from before that model came out.'

'That's the car,' Ian said shortly. He hurried downhill to his Land Rover and grabbed the radio mike. We followed more slowly, puzzled and anxious. I had an uneasiness in my stomach that I had not felt since the first labour pains. As I came within earshot I heard Ian say, 'Stay with the car. Try to be inconspicuous. If anyone goes near it, hold him. And call in. Have another car sent direct to the house.' He signed off. 'Fat chance on a Sunday,' he added to me.

'Ronnie?' Dad said.

'Coming,' said my uncle. They have known each other long enough to need few words.

'I'm going there now,' Ian said. 'You needn't—'

'If somebody is hanging around my house,' Dad said firmly, 'I am going to be there. You ladies carry on for the moment. And Wal,' he added.

There was an outcry as Mum, Janet and I made it clear that we were not going to be left in the wilderness, wondering what was going on, who was getting into trouble or danger and which of our precious possessions was going walkies. Dad shrugged and headed for Ronnie's Land Rover, the vehicle most suitable for slamming over the rough ground, and the least valuable.

'Well, all right,' Ian shouted after him. 'But *no guns!*'

Dad nodded, waved a hand and vanished. As I ran to join my husband at his Land Rover, I had time to look back. Mum had Bruce safe in his carrycot. I hoped that Dad's signal meant that he was concurring. He has been known to get rough when his family or his possessions are threatened.

Ian hustled down the track. I clung for dear life to whatever handholds I could find. Even so, Ronnie's Land Rover vanished rapidly from sight – hitting, as far as I could see, about every third bump; certainly, as it disappeared over the crest, I seemed to see a remarkable amount of daylight under it. Mum, with the family jeep, had waited to collect Triffid, Dad's old Labrador, and Bruce and then nursed the vehicle tenderly along. She was left far behind.

Much of my life had been spent being thrown around in a series of old and outdated Land Rovers driven by my uncle. It was a revelation to travel in one that had been maintained to police standards. The relative silence and the certainty that no bits were about to fall off it produced an unfamiliar sense of security. Ian used his klaxon and lights through the streets of Newton Lauder, but once he had a clear road he switched them off. 'What do you reckon?' he asked me. 'House or wood?'

I was so surprised to be consulted at all that it took me a quarter of a mile to work out what he meant. Then, 'House,' I said.

I had given Ian time to do some thinking of his own. 'No,' he said. 'Your father will think that way. No point in all of us fetching up at the house while the man I want is skulking in the woods.'

'You have two men at his car,' I pointed out.

'Young, inexperienced and unarmed. Your Mr Foster isn't exactly a tough cookie, but he may not be alone. Or he may be armed, which has the effect of stiffening the flabbiest spine. If he comes out of the woods brandishing a sawn-off shotgun, they'll radio for instructions. Or climb a tree.'

Suddenly, I wished that I had gone with Mother. Then I decided that if Ian was going to dash into danger, I wanted to be with him. Then I thought about Bruce and changed my mind back again. But it was far too late to do anything about it – or to do anything but hang on tight and hope for the best. Ian had passed the byroad to Briesland House and turned into the forestry track which ran through the woods in a roughly parallel direction. The mad bouncing had begun again. Evergreen branches slashed at the sides and a resinous smell filled the vehicle.

I glimpsed a panda car tucked away in a firebreak and the roof of Briesland House beyond. Ahead, in a small clearing, was Mr Foster's big Volvo. The scene was deserted but as we pulled to a halt two young uniformed constables – they looked young even to me – emerged from the fringe of the conifers. I saw Ian take a good look. But they could have been into the panda and blocking in the Volvo within a few seconds, so he made no criticism.

'Is that Foster's car?' he asked me.

'That's the one.' I looked in the Volvo. The back seats were flat but the car was empty except for a black and white dog of mixed parentage, which snarled at me from the front passenger seat.

'All quiet?' Ian asked the two men as they reached us.

'Not what you'd call quiet,' one of the constables said judiciously. 'A minute ago, there was a hell of a bang from just over there.' He pointed towards where the byroad to Briesland House ran, beyond the trees.

Ian frowned. He was reared in the old school of formal reporting and addressing one's senior as 'sir'. But

55

there were more urgent matters demanding attention. 'A shot?' he demanded.

The other constable shook his head. 'More like a car smash,' he said.

I was already into the forestry and trying to make speed through a jungle which seemed to have been designed to make progress impossible, but it would still be quicker that way than round by the road in the Land Rover. I heard Ian say 'Stay—' but the rest was lost in the brush of the needles against my clothes. I was forcing my way along a furrow. The spruce were about half grown and the going was hard to impossible. Within seconds I was soaked with sweat and prey to a million midges, and my clothes were full of spruce needles. I could hear Ian coming behind me.

At last I burst out of the trees and hurdled a fence which on an ordinary day I would have climbed with care. Two hundred yards to my right, where the drive of Briesland House led off at an angle, the empty byroad ran on towards the market garden. But when I looked to my left my heart lurched. An ancient Land Rover was in the ditch beyond the road, half on its side and half on its roof. It was badly crumpled against one of the beech trees which border the field. There was an unhealthy silence but for the clicks of a cooling exhaust and a regular squeak from a wheel which was still turning.

Ian erupted out of the trees and paused. 'Stand back,' he said. 'There could be fire.'

My mind was still working. 'It's a diesel,' I managed to gasp out. Ian himself had told me that diesel fuel is much less flammable than petrol and the diesel engine has no ignition wiring to provide a spark.

'Oh. Yes.'

We arrived together at the inverted vehicle. I could feel that my knees were loose but I hid the weakness from Ian.

What I saw was not quite as bad as my worst imaginings. Dad and Uncle Ronnie were tangled together against what would have been the passenger's window. One of them at least was moving but I could not tell which. Glass had broken. There was blood. I struggled to keep my head. It would not have been a good moment for the vapours and Mum had brought me up to stay calm in a crisis and save the hysterics for later.

Ian had made one quick and unsuccessful attempt to lift the upper door. The tailgate was jammed into the side of the ditch and the Land Rover had a metal roof. Ian had a personal radio in his hand – grabbed off one of the constables, I discovered later. He was already sending urgent messages to the emergency services.

My instinct was to stay there, perhaps helping the rescuers on by nothing more than applied willpower. But logically I knew that I would only be in the way and that if I gave in to the vapours I might even distract somebody from helping Dad. And there was one more thing. It was screaming for attention from somebody and I seemed to be the only person available.

As soon as we emerged from the rustle of forcing our way through the trees I had begun to receive another but less urgent signal. Dad and Uncle Ronnie were now both stirring sluggishly. Anxious as I was, I could do them no good by standing and gawking helplessly at them. I turned and ran towards the house. The yodel of the alarm system became louder and I saw that the strobe light was flashing under the eaves. It came as no surprise to see that the front door had been forced and was standing wide.

I leaned against the door jamb for a full minute. I was gasping for breath. Having babies takes it out of one rather. When I could breathe without feeling that my lungs would burst into flames, I took a few seconds to kill the alarms. The silence was better than an anthem. I did not want to go further. But in the end I pulled myself together and climbed the stairs. I went slowly. There was no hurry now.

A small charge had been used to blow open the steel-lined door of Dad's workroom. After years of being greeted by the array of superlative workmanship – for man has always devoted a disproportionate amount of time, effort and resources to weaponry and transport – the bareness was an appalling affront. It took only one swift glance inside to show me that every gun had gone. They had even stripped the walls of the few other weapons – the two samurai swords, the beautiful Malayan kris, the dirks, others which I could not remember for the moment.

Almost every gun, I corrected myself. They had missed the smaller gun-safe built into a cupboard below part of the workbench. They might regret the careless-ness, I thought grimly. It held a number of modern handguns.

Chapter Four

For the moment it seemed that firearms had no part to play – fortunately, because I was quite angry enough to have blown somebody's head off. The enemy had gone.

Just across the landing was a bathroom. I hurried inside. I wanted to vomit but in the end I only washed and came out again, hurrying down the stairs. I pulled the front door as close to as its splintered stile allowed. As I jogged back to the capsized Land Rover, I told myself that neither Dad nor my uncle would have died – please God – but that if something ghastly had indeed happened it would not have been because I had left the scene.

The emergency services had not had far to come. Even so, either they had not wasted a second or else I had been away for longer than I thought. A fire appliance and an ambulance were blocking the byroad. The Land Rover had already been opened up like a can of beans and the firemen were standing by while at the same time packing up their gear.

Dad was on a stretcher near the open rear door of the ambulance. One of the paramedics was doing something to a splint on his left leg. Above Dad's eye was a swelling lump surmounted by a bad gash. The bleeding had stopped but his face was streaked with dark scarlet.

Amazingly, his sunglasses were still in place, unbroken and only slightly bent. The other ambulanceman was inside what was left of the Land Rover, attending to my uncle. I was relieved to hear the steady rumble of Uncle Ronnie's voice.

I stooped over my father. I nearly asked whether he was all right, but I had the sense to ask him instead, 'Dad, how do you feel?'

'I'll make it,' he said. His voice was soft. I guessed that he had already been given something to deaden the pain, but even so I could see that breathing was painful for him. 'How's Ron?' he asked.

'From the way he's swearing, he'll make it too. He'll have to. If he dies now, he'll never go to heaven.'

Dad smiled faintly. 'They won't have him anyway.' Then I saw him make an effort and concentrate his mind. 'You've been to the house? So Ian said. What's the damage?'

'Don't worry about it just now,' I said.

A trace of the old fire flickered in his eyes. He could hardly speak above a whisper but there was a bite in his voice. 'You needn't talk to me as if I was your bairn instead of the other way round. I'll worry if I want to. So tell me.'

I glanced at the ambulanceman, who shrugged. 'He'll worry more if you keep him in the dark,' he said.

'It's not good,' I told Dad.

'They cleaned me out?'

I nodded.

'Just the gunroom?'

I nodded again.

'Christ!' he breathed. 'I'm sorry, Toots. There goes most of your inheritance.'

That statement was hard to take in. The guns, I had always known, were valuable; but our lifestyle, though not luxurious, had been comfortable enough to give me a sense of solidity and permanence. 'I don't understand,' I said. 'You still have the house and the business. You looked on those guns as your personal collection.'

'Only some of them,' he said. 'And I still owe a bundle on those. Some of the guns are stock. Some belong to clients. My God! I took in a pair of Holland and Hollands only yesterday, for re-bluing and adjusting the trigger-pulls.'

'The insurance will take care of it,' I said soothingly.

'Not by a mile,' he said, with his eyes closed behind his shades. 'Have you any idea what full insurance would have cost? I thought our precautions were good enough. And the Clunes' two Scottish long guns were beyond price. I'm wiped out, near as dammit.'

The paramedic in the Land Rover called for help in getting Uncle Ron out. His mate and two firemen went to join him. They struggled to lift the big frame out and onto a stretcher.

'At least they didn't get the modern handguns,' I told Dad. 'The gun-safe hadn't been touched.'

I knew at once that I'd said the wrong thing. 'It gets worse and worse,' he told me. 'That Wildey, point four five magnum, gas-operated semi-auto that I ordered turned up the other day. I test-fired it last night. Very accurate but a hellish recoil. I left it out on the bench, along with what was left of a box of ammunition, meaning to clean it tonight. It's gone?'

'I certainly didn't see it.' I needed to know more, but all that we had managed so far had been to exchange bad news. 'Dad, exactly what happened to you? Does it hurt to talk?'

'Not a lot.' The painkiller was taking effect but was making it more difficult for him to concentrate. I saw him making an effort. 'We decided to head straight for the house. A good guess but a bad idea as it happened. We hadn't thought it out.' He paused and swallowed. I would have fetched water for him except that I felt sure that it was important that I got his story right away. 'They were coming away from the house in a van, not very big but heavy, solidly built, moving fast. We seemed to be converging at about a zillion miles an hour. Ronnie was driving. If I'd had the wheel, I'd have pulled up and baled out, taking the key with me. That would have boxed them in. But Ronnie didn't see it that way. First he tried to bluff it out. Even when it was obvious that they were coming on, he kept going. Well, the Land Rover may be – have been – solid but it would never have been a match for that . . . tank. At the last moment, he swerved—'

'Take it easy,' I said. Dad was sweating but he was very white. Ian had come to stand beside me. I reached up and took the handkerchief out of his breast pocket and mopped Dad's face.

'How can I take it easy?' he asked petulantly. 'Do you realize—?'

'I think I do. But it may not be too late to do something.'

'Can you get them back?'

'I can try,' I said. 'And Ian has the law to help him. But I wish you were fit to take over. So, no promises, but we'll do our damnedest. Go on – quickly, before they take you away. Describe the van.'

'I don't remember looking at it,' Dad said. 'I was too busy seeing my past life flash by.' He paused. 'It had a name on it. Somebody's van hire. MacBean, perhaps.'

'Or Maclean,' said Ronnie's voice. They put his stretcher down beside us while they recovered from the effort of lifting all that bone and muscle.

'It was grey,' Dad said.

'Nah,' Ronnie said. His voice was getting stronger by the minute. 'It was blue.'

'Grey,' Dad said. 'I think. We're not being much help. Listen, Toots. Do something.'

He said it so seriously that I thought that he had decided on a course of action. 'Do what?' I asked.

'How do I know? Something clever. You're my girl.'

I lifted the sunglasses off his nose. He looked worse without them. The blood had run behind them and made a puddle around his eye. The paramedics, who had got their breaths back, tried to shoo me away. Despite the anaesthetic, Dad had his wits about him. 'Listen,' he said, 'what happened to the Bentons?'

Before I could reply, Mum arrived. She still had Triffid with her and, I was pleased to see, Bruce, but she had delayed to set down Janet and Wallace. Wal's pulse had accelerated slightly during the excitement and Janet had insisted on taking him home.

Mum is one of the calmest and least flappable people I know, but with her husband and her brother both on stretchers beside a Land Rover which had been wrenched asunder – by the fire brigade rather than by impact or a bomb, although she was not to know that – she switched instantly into her inquisitorial mode. She wanted to know considerably more about what had happened to the patients and why and when, and just what their conditions and prognoses might be, than the two paramedics were qualified to answer. The two stretchers were stowed in the ambulance. At that point, Mum suddenly announced that she was going to travel with the patients and overcame any protests by simply not listening.

Dad's last message before the doors were closed, aimed at whoever it might concern which really meant me, was that the pheasant poults could be spread among the old pens if they arrived before the new one was finished. I had to back the jeep into a field to let the ambulance turn in the same gate. Then we were left to pick up the pieces.

My mind was fizzing with all the conflicting demands that were being made on it.

Ian still had the constable's radio in his hand. I had heard the intermittent mutter of his voice as he kept Control informed and requested backup. At the moment, Control seemed to be stalling on the matter of backup while asking him many questions that he could not possibly answer. 'That van—' he said to me. 'Which are we to believe? Can you make a guess?'

It was for that purpose that I had taken Dad's amber shades. I wiped off some blood with Ian's handkerchief and put them on. The reds and greens became brighter but the blue sky became grey. 'I think my uncle got it right,' I told Ian. 'The van was blue. Dad's glasses made it look grey to him.' Ian passed the information on.

'Can you get that car brought round here?' I asked him.

'Maybe. You mustn't touch anything,' he added quickly.

'I'm not daft and I know the drill. But what about the dog?'

'From the signs, it's more likely to touch you,' said my unfeeling husband. 'But Constable Morpeth can cope. He's always telling his colleagues how all dogs take to him.'

While he gave directions over the radio I tried again to order my thoughts. What came first? I remembered Dad's penultimate message. When I had Ian's attention again, I said, 'Somebody should go along to the market garden and make sure that the Bentons are all right.'

Ian looked puzzled. Nobody had ever told him about our eccentric alarm system. A thousand other things were screaming for my attention but I took time to explain. 'Your colleagues don't like private alarm systems permanently connected to them,' I told him rapidly, 'and, anyway, our phone wires are above ground and would be easily cut. So we have an arrangement with the Bentons who have the market garden at the end of this byroad. If our alarm goes off, they phone the police unless they hear from us straight away that it's a false alarm.'

'So what went wrong?'

'That's what we want to know. While Mr Foster was here, a starling triggered the alarm system and Dad mentioned phoning the Bentons. I could see him kicking himself afterwards.'

'They could be out.'

'There are about four generations of them, including several babies. They're never all out at the same time. And Joe Benton has a mobile phone.'

65

Ian took it seriously. He borrowed the jeep. I was just in time to rescue Bruce and Triffid before he shot off in the direction of the market garden, talking into the radio while he drove. I lugged what seemed to be a hundred-weight of baby along to Briesland House, in through the broken front door and put him down in the kitchen. A puzzled Triffid followed at heel. He had never seen so many strange goings-on.

Over the next hour and more I came as near as is humanly possible to doing a dozen things simultaneously while still thinking several steps ahead. I changed Bruce. I dashed upstairs and took a look from the window of the ravaged workroom. The panda car was visible through a chink in the trees, which explained why Mr Foster had not returned for his Volvo. I phoned the local joiner to come and execute emergency repairs. I reached an impasse with Directory Enquiries.

Ian, looking more angry than ever, came back to say that the Bentons had been attacked and tied up, all but the babies, but otherwise were not much damaged. Their attackers, three in number, had been armed and masked.

Ian was waiting for me to comment, but what I had to say I would say later to the Bentons. When instead I asked Ian for the surname of ex-Chief Superintendent Munro's married sister, he looked at me bug-eyed but gave it to me, from memory, dashing off immediately. Either he was too busy to waste precious time in argument, or he trusted me totally, or else he thought that I had cracked under the strain. Some day I may face up to asking him.

I resumed my wrestling match with Directory Enquiries, but one submission and a pinfall later I had the

number that I wanted. Mr Munro had put off his retirement until the last permissible moment. When he was at
last put out to grass, instead of returning to his native
Hebrides he had settled down with his widowed sister
somewhere in the Grampian Region. He was a long, lean,
dark Highlander with a Calvinistic attitude to life and a
pathological hatred of firearms. He and Dad had been
poles apart in the human spectrum and yet they had
dealt almost amicably, off and on, for a number of years.
Mr Munro had always looked favourably on Ian and had,
I thought modestly, a soft spot for myself. His sister
answered the phone and went to find him.

A few precious seconds spent in friendly chat were
inescapable but I cut them to the polite minimum. When
I told him what had happened, he was appalled. No
matter that most of the guns were too old or too valuable
to shoot, guns were guns and they had been stolen. He
was also concerned for Dad. I gave him a moderately
optimistic report on Dad's condition and told him what I
wanted. He promised action straight away.

The Volvo had arrived at the door. Neither the dog
nor the alarms and devices had been sufficient to thwart
a trained officer and I wondered how many of them
became crooks in retirement. The officer – Constable
Morpeth, I assumed correctly – was standing safely on
the gravel, being barked at through the glass. So much, I
thought, for his vaunted knack with dogs. But he seemed
unmarked and I gave him full marks for courage. To drive
a car with the owner's dog snarling in one's ear must take
guts. I had just made up a bottle for Bruce so I carried
them both outside. Bruce ignored the Volvo – the car fixa-
tion would come later, I supposed – and sucked frantically

at the teat while I walked twice round the car, watched by Constable Morpeth and, of course, the dog.

'Open the tailgate, please,' I asked Morpeth.

'The dog could get out . . .'

'Not a chance,' I told him. 'That's his territory and he'll stick to it.'

Morpeth looked doubtful but he did as I asked. Carefully, using a clean handkerchief, he lifted the rear door. He had had the preservation of evidence drummed into him but I could not see that an extra set of Foster's fingerprints would have helped very much. A wisp of what I took to be thistledown detached itself from the hinge and wafted away on the slight breeze. The dog stayed put. 'Lift the rubber mat,' I said.

'But—'

'I'm not going to touch anything. You are.'

He must have decided that an inspector's wife had some delegated authority because, using a ballpoint pen, he rolled the mat back. The original carpet had been cut and there was a solid-looking lid to whatever box had been welded under the floor. But although there was a security lock, the key had not been turned and Morpeth managed to lift the lid at the expense of breaking his pen. The box was empty except for a scrap of paper. The printing was faint but I managed to read part of it.

'That's all at this end,' I said. 'Open the front passenger door. I'm going to take that dog out.'

'I wouldn't,' he said. 'The dog—'

I nearly said something very rude about the dog. I had been brought up with dogs and I could hardly remember a time when there had not been at least one young dog in training. All the body language of this specimen suggested threat and bluff rather than active aggression. Even so I felt a prickle of atavistic fear as Morpeth, still protesting, opened the door. I handed him Bruce and the bottle, just to keep him occupied.

The dog made a pretence of being on the point of attack . . . until I picked up the lead which was lying on the dash. The holder of the leash was the leader of the pack. Immediately, it became my slave. I attached the lead and out it came. Or rather, out he came, as I could see as soon as he moved.

The Constable was unhappy. 'Inspector Fellowes said that he'd have my guts if I let you take anything,' he almost wailed.

'This is a dog, not a thing,' I pointed out. 'Do you suppose that my husband really meant you to leave the dog to starve, or to roast in the sun? He's forgotten the poor mutt, if I haven't. He'll be here if he's wanted.'

I recovered Bruce, now sound asleep, and entered the house, carrying the baby in one arm, leading the dog with the other hand and carrying the bottle under that armpit. I just managed to deposit Bruce, fairly gently, in his carrycot before it was time to avert a dogfight. Of the two, Triffid was the aggressor but he backed down when he saw me raise the chain end of the lead. The newcomer drank deeply from Triffid's bowl. We did not want an outbreak of canine fleas so I went over him quickly with the comb, to his great pleasure. There were no fleas but I came on a sheep-tick on his neck. I rubbed it with Vaseline and then rotated it anticlockwise until, dizzied, it lost its grip and fell to the floor. I was about to tread on it when I had a further thought. I found a tiny clean bottle, once a whisky miniature, and scooped the nasty little bag of blood into it. The two dogs settled at opposite ends of the kitchen, showing each other the whites of their eyes.

The light on the answering machine was blinking, indicating a message. It was from Janet, wanting to know what was going on. Well, she could wait. I phoned the Bentons, intending to make a polite enquiry, but got no answer. They had probably been removed to hospital, babies and all, while they recovered from shock.

What next? I wondered.

One of my several trains of thought began to gel. Mum had recently produced a set of reins left over from my childhood, ready for whenever Bruce began to toddle. I hunted them out and jingled the little bells. In an instant, Foster's dog was sitting at my feet, eyes alight. It was a similar reaction to one that I had seen a thousand times, that of a gun dog to the snap of a shotgun's action closing. I nodded to myself.

The house was quiet. The Constable and the Volvo had vanished. Suddenly I did not like being alone. There was no reason why anyone should come back, I told myself firmly, but then I remembered the dog. Mr Foster might or might not be a dog person, but I knew that Dad or I would have gone back into hell to recover a favourite dog. I braved the bareness of the workroom and keyed the combination on the small gun-safe. I hesitated for a moment at the Ceska Zbrojovka CZ 1950 but passed it by, accepting instead the heavier weight of the Belgian-made Browning Hi-Power in exchange for the larger calibre and 13-shot magazine. Along with it I took a spare magazine and a heavy little box of 9 mm. Parabellum ammunition down to Dad's study. With the pistol out of the box, loaded and at my elbow, and two dogs in the house, I felt safer. I tackled the computer.

Calling the list of antique weaponry out of the memory was easy – it was Dad's habit to update it after every sale or purchase. I had to go upstairs again, with the Browning for company, and fetch the daybook to find out what clients' guns had been brought in recently. As I added them to the list I tried very hard not to guess at the total value of the haul, but habit dies hard. The figure that kept sneaking into my mind terrified me. Even allowing for the guns which Dad had deliberately overpriced, the total came to almost a million. I made several printouts.

There was nothing on the computer yet about insurance but I found a file in a desk drawer. The latest figure for our cover was substantial, but it would cover less than half the value of the stolen guns.

What would Dad do? I wondered. Would he try to keep the robbery a secret? Or would he broadcast it far and wide, making transport and disposal more difficult at the risk of attracting every vulture looking for pickings? But the news would leak anyway. Better to slam as many doors as possible. I prepared a circular to Dad's list of clients, which comprised most of the major collectors and museums, to be sent by fax and e-mail. The trade would soon pick it up or be circulated by the police. On my own initiative I made mention of a substantial reward.

I phoned Dad's insurers, avoiding any mention of the total value of the loss. Unless we were both lucky and clever, sooner or later the question of under-insurance would rear its head. The insurers promised to send a claim form. Mum arrived home by taxi before the call finished. I told the machine to send out the messages and then to disconnect. I could hear it dialling out as I left the room. Mum was preparing food, as she usually does when perturbed. I suddenly realized that I had not eaten since breakfast and was rapidly starving to death. I hid the pistol in the hallstand glovebox and joined her in the kitchen for news and food.

The cuts and bruises, Mum said, had turned out to be superficial by hospital standards. I had been afraid that my uncle, who had been removed from the Land Rover with the aid of a cutting device, might be badly damaged; but it turned out that he had been trapped by the foot between the pedals and had suffered no more than a badly sprained ankle. He would be released next day, they thought. Personally, I was sure of it. They would be sick of him by morning and he was not the type to succumb to delayed shock.

'And Dad?' I asked.

'Your father,' Mum said sternly, 'was not wearing his seat belt, so let it be a lesson to you. He's broken a collarbone and several ribs and he got a dunt on one kneecap that they don't think has broken it – nothing showed on X-ray – but they can't be sure. They think he'll be in there for at least a week. And they can keep him,' Mum added ambiguously.

She had made tea, toast and boiled eggs, always our immediate solace in times of trouble. I fell to ravenously. 'You've been upstairs?' I asked with my mouth full.

'Just a quick look,' she said. 'They don't seem to have been anywhere except your Dad's workroom, so that's all right.'

I chewed and swallowed hastily, laying the foundation for later heartburn. 'How can it be all right?' I demanded.

'I couldn't have borne it if they'd gone through all my things,' she said simply.

'Dad says that not all the guns were ours and the insurance won't cover it.'

'Just so long as the insurance covers other people's guns,' Mum said, 'I'll be satisfied. So we'll have lost the value of the oldies. So what? As long as we have the house and the business, we'll get by.'

Her placidity was irritating while I was so worried. But Mum had lived for most of her life secure in the usually justified belief that Dad would always find a magic wand to wave. The magician's mantle seemed to have fallen on my shoulders and I could feel the weight of it pressing me down. But there would have been no point in spoiling her serenity before it was necessary.

And I held back for another reason. For many years, while Mum was engaged with her own affairs, I had spent every free moment with Dad, 'following him around like a puppy' as Mum said, watching him at work and learning the ins and outs of the gun trade, laying the foundation on which my own involvement in the family business was later built. I had accompanied him shooting, worked ferrets for him and helped with the training of gun dogs when he was too busy. As a result, I had spent more waking time with him than Mum had, and while I was not privy to all his little secrets I was aware that he had a source of loan capital about which he wanted my mother to know nothing. From hints dropped by Uncle Wal, I gathered that he had, at some time long past, done a big favour for a business of a less than reputable nature, and the loans were his continuing reward. They were at a very low rate of interest; but they were loans, not gifts. And a debt is still a debt. I hated the novel idea of a load of debts poised over the family, but Mum would have hated it more and I found myself feeling more protective than ever in the past.

I finished eating in silence, or as much silence as is possible while munching on an apple, and went back to the study. The fax machine had garnered a second message from Janet, insisting that I phone her at the shop. She would be waiting there while Wallace had his rest, intending to give him a heavily expurgated version of events.

I was speaking to Janet when Ian came in. I finished my report to her in remarkably few words while he went to Mum for a share of the food. He came back chewing and carrying a mug. I gave him a copy of my printout and he faxed it to Edinburgh for the Stolen List.

'Now it's just a matter of waiting,' he said, sitting back in one of the leather chairs. 'We've done all that we can.' He at least appreciated the size of the disaster that had ocurred, but he was steeped in the police philosophy of allowing routine to produce the answers.

I, on the other hand, had learned from Dad that corners can be cut and issues forced. 'Wrong,' I said. 'Wrong, wrong, wrong! We haven't done a half, not a tenth, of what we can.'

'You think so?' He cogitated in silence for long enough to finish his first sandwich. 'I don't see what more we can do until we get another lead.'

'If I can get a lead, could you get away to help me hunt?'

He laughed without showing any sign of amusement. 'Not a hope in hell! Your father has trodden on too many toes. I don't know how having the toes trodden on can give you a red face,' he said thoughtfully, 'but it's happened more than once. I've spoken to Edinburgh. They tut-tutted, but I had the feeling that they saw it as poetic justice that he should get ripped off. They'll do what's required by proper procedures, but their hearts won't be in it. And the uniformed super here takes his orders from Edinburgh.'

'Could you get leave?'

'I could try,' he said doubtfully. 'I have some leave due me.' He bit an enormous hot dog. Mum had decided long since that he needed building up.

I remembered the Land Rover and called the garage to come and remove the remains. Ian's radio was quacking and he went outside to take the call with his mouth still full. When I hung up, the phone rang immediately.

It was Mr Munro. He already had most of what I had asked, plus an invitation from his sister to come and visit. 'And will young Sergeant Fellowes be coming with you?' I said that I very much wanted him with me but explained that Ian, despite now being an inspector, was having difficulty in getting away.

'Just you leave that with me,' he said. 'Who has charge in Newton Lauder these days?'

'Mr McKnight has your old job,' I said.

'Does he indeed?' I heard him cackle with laughter. The sound carried me back. Over the years I had not heard him laugh aloud very often, but once heard the sound was not easily forgotten. 'He has me to thank for his promotion,' he said. 'I will speak to him.'

While we talked, I had remembered that although the Land Rover belonged to my uncle's employer, it was his responsibility to insure it and he had gone to the same firm. When the line was clear I called the insurers. They were not pleased to hear my voice again but a second claim form was promised.

I followed Ian outside, caught him as a radio call finished and handed him the small bottle. 'I took this tick off the dog,' I told him. 'It might tell us something. If the previous host was a red deer, for instance, or a grouse—'

'Do sheep-ticks batten on to grouse?'

'Certainly they do. They're believed to carry louping-ill,' I explained. 'I know it's a forlorn sort of hope but it might at least go towards confirming some other pointer. Just might. It's a thin chance, like asking a pathologist to determine what a corpse had eaten three days before death, long after stomach acid and enzymes have done their worst.'

Ian looked through the glass at the little bladder of blood with its tiny legs. 'Maybe,' he said. 'They can't have as sophisticated a metabolism as we do. It's worth a try. There's a professor in Edinburgh who's at the forefront of DNA research and he's speeded up the processes. I'm told that he loves a challenge. We may as well give him one.'

I went back to the kitchen in search of more food. It had been a long day and it was far from over. Mum had fed both dogs and was nursing Bruce.

I was finishing a second snack when Ian came in, radio in hand. He looked at me, bemused. 'I seem to be on leave, as from now,' he said.

'How convenient,' I said. The food had renewed my

energy and I was raring to go. 'We're going north. I'll explain once we're on the road. We'd better return your Land Rover and fetch our car. Mum, will you keep Bruce for a few days?'

The pleasure on her face was answer enough.

Chapter Five

I gave Mum almost a dozen guarded messages for Dad and as many instructions for Bruce's well-being. (Admittedly she had managed to bring me safely to adult-hood, but I had always suspected that that had been a bit of a fluke.) While Ian was saying his goodbyes to Bruce, I borrowed Mum's largest handbag and smuggled the Browning out to the Land Rover. Since joining the family, Ian has learned to handle a shotgun very competently but he has never learned to accept firearms anywhere but in strictly controlled conditions.

Ian dropped me along with the dog at our flat and I transferred the pistol in its box to beneath the passenger's seat of our car. I put a cushion on the back seat for the dog who, I had decided for no particular reason, I would rename Mac.

Then I packed for both of us. I showered and changed to the skin – my clothes of the day were ripped and dirty and, anyway, would have been unsuitable. I loaded the car, turned off the boiler, locked up and headed down to the police building behind the Town Hall. Days are long in the Scottish summer, but the sun was low and russet and the shadows were lengthening.

Ian had had time to clear his desk and hand over his

part in the official investigation. Before I had even parked the car, he came out of the building carrying the sort of small case without which no detective feels complete and opened the boot. 'What the hell?' he said.

I knew what he meant. I had stowed our two shotguns in the boot. 'You never know when they may come in useful,' I said weakly.

He took over the wheel. 'I hope you mean that we'll be free to shoot a few clays or go after the rabbits.'

'Yes, of course,' I said.

'You'd better mean that.' At the Square, he slowed.

'North, you said?' he asked patiently.

On a quick mental review of the past hour I realized that I had been too busy and too psyched-up to spare time for explanations. Ian had trusted me. 'That's right,' I said. 'We're heading north. We're going to visit your ex-boss.'

Ian complied. 'Which ex-boss?' he asked. 'I seem to have had hundreds.' It was probably true. He was subject to his CID chiefs in Edinburgh but administratively he came under the chief superintendent in Newton Lauder.

'Ex-Chief Superintendent Munro,' I told him. 'He's expecting us, so don't hang about.'

Obligingly, Ian put his foot down. We emerged onto one of the main roads between Edinburgh and Newcastle. Traffic was heavy while the use of headlamps in the failing light made driving a matter for concentration. We were following a coach up Soutra before Ian relaxed and said, 'Don't you think that you should explain?'

'Yes, of course,' I said. 'I was waiting until you could spare some attention from the road. What did you get from the Volvo's registration?'

'That combination was never issued. They're trying to track the car from chassis and engine numbers, but that takes longer. What do you care about the registration?'

'Only this. The first thing that seemed to me to be out of key about Mr Foster was that the registration year-letter didn't fit the age of the car. It's an Aberdeen registration.'

'That doesn't mean anything – it's fictitious,' Ian said. I felt the car slow.

'All the same, where would Aberdeen plates be least conspicuous?' (The car picked up again.) 'And the tax disc was issued in Aberdeen. The disc may have been stolen and altered, but the connection remains. Mrs Shaw said that she thought he had an accent from further north. "Between the Tay and the Moray Firth" was how she put it. But you know how the telephone strengthens an accent. When I heard him on the phone, it screamed "Grampian" at me.'

Ian followed the coach onto the roof of the Lammermuirs and then overtook. 'That doesn't mean that he's based there now,' he said doggedly. 'He told you that he was living abroad.'

'Just the sort of story he would tell. I caught him flat-footed, just as Dad did on the phone. Do you, as a detective, always have to have solid proof to start with? Or do you accept an accumulation of pointers?'

'Pointers, if there are enough of them,' Ian admitted.

'Then add this one to the rest. You heard what Dad and my uncle said about the van?'

'Most of it.'

'Mr Munro looked in the Yellow Pages for me. He

says that there's a firm in Aberdeen, McBean's Van Hire.
He thinks that their vans are blue.'

Ian was nodding as he drove. 'It adds up,' he said.
'Just a little bit.'

'Then add this,' I told him. 'I touched nothing, but I
persuaded your bobby to open the tailgate, very carefully,
and roll back the rubber matting. There was a specially
built, lockable compartment, just as we thought. It was
unlocked and he managed to open it without spoiling any
clues, if there were any. All that was in the compartment
was a scrap of paper. It was one of those cash register
slips that people insist on giving you just to fill up your
handbag or pockets. Your colleagues will probably find it
tomorrow or the day after, but they won't tell you because
you're on leave. But the point is that the place of origin
was just about legible. It said *Cocket Hat Filling Station*.
Where do you suppose that would be?'

I waited for an answer which I already knew.

'Aberdeen,' Ian said. The car picked up more speed
and began slicing through the going-home traffic.

Police training had honed Ian's natural ability as a
driver. He was fast but safe. In what seemed very little
time, we were on the ring road around Edinburgh. By
then, I was beginning to look for flaws in my own logic.
'Why would he be based up in Grampian?' I asked Ian
suddenly. 'Surely he'd need to be near his customers.'

'Not necessarily.'

Ian was lost in thought for some miles – wondering,
I guessed later, just how much I should be told. We were
nearing the great arc of lights that was the Forth Bridge,
with more lights of North Queensferry and Rosyth

dancing in the water, before he made up his mind. 'He isn't a seller, he's a buyer.'

I thought that that was all that was coming, but after he had paid the bridge toll and wound up his window again, he resumed. 'I had a long phone call from one of the big wheels after we reported our first suspicions. He told me some background. He was so pleased to have a useful lead at last that he opened up a bit. They know that, whoever he is, he isn't a one-man band. You see, there are two specialist intelligence units whose main, almost only, function is to keep an eye open for bribery and corruption.'

'Are there really!'

It was an exclamation rather than a question, but he answered it. 'Yes, there are really. In England it's a section with a computer and one foot in the Treasury, the other in Scotland Yard. Proper title the Standard Supervisory Department. Up here it's the Personal Income Investigation Branch, comprising two men and a girl with a card index somewhere near St Andrews House, but those in the know refer to it as the Sleaze Squeeze.

'They have powers to compel banks and other financial bodies to disgorge information and their remit is to monitor the lifestyles of people in a position to be tempted to corruption or fraud.'

'That could be a hell of a lot of people,' I said.

'It is. Current indications are that there are two buyers – Foster covering Scotland and the north of England and another man doing the rest of England plus Wales. And somewhere there are other men, probably the bosses, who have clout and inside gen. They single out the takers of funny money – perhaps even persuade the vulnerable into it – show them how to explain it away and provide them with valuable antiques to be "discovered". As an alternative, they may seek out the givers of the bribes and start the deal from that end. Those are the men they want most.'

'Could the one client that they know about, thanks to us – Leonard James White – not point the finger at one of them?'

'Could, yes. Will, probably, in the fullness of time. Does, not yet. He's too scared. Unpleasant things have happened to the few who've contributed scraps of information.

'So, to come back to your question, the purchasing agent for North Britain wants to be out of the public eye, yet handy to carrier services, airport, railway and outlets to America and the Continent.'

'They have links?'

'It seems so. Looking at it that way, since the arrival of all the oil industry traffic Grampian fills the bill as well as anywhere. If it happens to be also his home territory . . .'

I used a little more thinking time. We crossed the bridge and set off along the motorway. 'Would there really be enough market to make it worth the while of so many men?' I asked at last.

'Think about it,' Ian said. 'Think how many people are tempted to, and probably do, accept money illegally for favours returned. Politicians and policemen. Stockbrokers and civil servants. Sportsmen. Disk jockeys. Planning officers. Tax officials. Insurance officers. MOT approved garages. Anyone with purchases to make or contracts to award or manage. The list is endless. And the signs are there. Since the authorities became sceptical about gambling wins, there have been a remarkable number of valuable finds by just that category of people. Several of them had the bloody nerve to have them "discovered" on the *Antiques Roadshow*. Mr Foster and his friends need never have been out of work.'

'Then surely there must be enough evidence?' I suggested.

'Not by a mile. Until recently, the explanation that Auntie's favourite teapot turned out to be Meissen of a very rare and collectable pattern was accepted at face value. Then it began to seem too good to be true. But people do still find Fabergé eggs in Granny's bottom drawer. How do we know which one is a genuine find? Only,' Ian said, answering his own question, 'when some prat makes a misjudgement and a falsified provenance comes round in a full circle. Otherwise, the "finder" only has to stick to a well-prepared story.'

That gave me a lot more food for thought and I disliked what I was thinking. It seemed that we had been playing with rough company and were planning to play some more. The thought of the guns in the car was some slight comfort. There was silence until we were near the end of the motorway. 'Which way are you going?' I asked

He hesitated for a moment. To reach Deeside from the south, you can take a long way round or choose from two roads over the mountains. 'Cairn o' Mount,' he said. 'At least we'll have dual carriageway for most of the distance.'

We passed the exit for Perth and Braemar. It was almost full darkness. Ian is easily dazzled, probably because of the paperwork entailed in his job and the consequent eye strain. 'Shall I take over?' I asked.

'Would you? I seem to have been dashing around since dawn.'

'Haven't we all? Never mind,' I said, 'I've had a rest and I can have another when you take over again.'

We had left the motorway. He stopped at the first lay-by and we exchanged seats. He lowered his seatback and before we reached Dundee he was dozing.

The Kingsway was quiet and soon we were bowling north again on the A94. When I glanced left I saw that Ian was asleep – deeply asleep, to judge from his breathing. Well, I thought, let him have his rest. He had put in a lot of hours recently – dogsbodying, as he put it, for his Edinburgh superiors over a case which had only a peripheral connection with the Borders. And now we were eating into his precious allocation of leave and landing another burden on him. I stopped at Stracathro for petrol and he never stirred. Rather than wake him, I decided to tackle the Cairn o' Mount.

I turned off. The easy road began to twist after Fetter-cairn. Then it climbed. The car laboured and I had to change down and down again. Low cloud made patchy fog on the high tops. I am not a fast driver over difficult and unfamiliar roads. Several times a car would come up behind me, wait its chance and then spurt past, so I was not surprised when the lights of another and taller vehicle settled in my mirror.

Ian stirred and stretched. 'Where have we got to?' he asked thickly.

'We're on the Cairn o' Mount. We passed the crest a few minutes ago.'

'You've done a good stint. Not far now. I'll take the wheel whenever you've had enough.'

We were on a long descent. I had not been on that road for years, and then only as a passenger, but I was watching out for a narrow stone bridge and a very sharp turn to the left before another climb. It was, I remembered, an accident waiting for the next careless driver.

The lights behind came closer. I slowed and pulled left to let him overtake if he could. I decided that I would let Ian have the wheel after that. Suddenly my lights showed the bridge ahead. The shadow of our car, thrown by the main beams of the vehicle behind us, grew to spread over the whole area. A moment later, the car was hit from behind and shunted forward. I stood on the brakes. Tyres howled, but the other vehicle was much heavier than ours and had the advantage of the hill. I could hear its engine struggling to push us ever faster.

The bridge was coming closer at frightening speed and the steering was precarious. I tried to ignore the crumpling sound behind me and the *What the hell?* noises from Ian and think my way out of trouble in the second or two that remained. I could continue as I was doing and probably be smashed against the parapet of the bridge or the bank beyond. I could try to accelerate clear of the other vehicle and take the bend at an impossible speed. Or . . .

At the last instant, I saw another option. I could not call it good but it was the least worst. I hauled on the wheel and gave one brief kick on the throttle. The pursuing vehicle struck us one last blow that actually helped us round. And then we were through the fence and bouncing over heather. It swished beneath the car and I had time to hope that the hot exhaust would not start a fire. We were on the bank of the Water of Dye, with the stream on our left and a steep rise on the other side. I stabbed at the brakes and missed, so I hauled right and we came to a halt. I switched off the lights and the night went very dark.

'Jesus!' Ian said. 'That had to be deliberate.' He was still half asleep but at least I was relieved to note that he was not blaming me. The dog in the back set up a frantic whining. He had my sympathy.

The car had slewed half round. To my right and rather behind my shoulder I could see the lights of the other vehicle. It had stopped beyond the bridge. Partly silhouetted against its own lights, it looked like one of the biggest Japanese 4WDs, perhaps a pick-up with hard-top added, but I was far from certain. What I could be sure of was that it had not stopped to offer help. And I remembered the pistol that had been stolen along with the antiques. My knees had turned to blancmange, but I could manage without them for the moment.

I groped beneath Ian's knees. The box had jumped forward and I found it at once. I opened it on my knee and, fumbling in the dark, went through the familiar motions of slapping in a magazine and cocking the action. My door seemed to have jammed. I wound the window down.

The men – there seemed to be three of them – were jogging back along the road, visible against the reflected glow of the lights. I was recovering my night vision. Each of the men was carrying something. I heard one voice say '. . . all right . . .' and another said, 'We'd better make sure they're bloody not.'

'We're under attack,' I told Ian. 'See if you can get out one of the shotguns.' Ian made the sort of inarticulate sound to be expected of a police officer when asked to break all the rules. I wasted no time in argument. I called out, 'Halt or I fire.'

Somebody laughed. They came on.

It was not a moment for hesitating, nor for pandering to the inhibitions of a dedicated policeman. In two minutes, Bruce might be an orphan. If it turned out to have been a genuine accident and they had indeed stopped to help, I could always apologize to any survivors.

Dad had taught me to shoot almost anything shootable before I was into my teens and I had hit running rabbits with the Browning before I was out of them; but the men were moving in darkness and were awkwardly positioned for my right hand. My first three or four shots did no damage. The sound of the shots was almost lost among the hills and the flashes killed most of my returning night vision. But then one of the bullets hit a rock and whined very satisfactorily away into the night.

There were sounds of consternation and the dimly seen figures began to recede. There would be no justification in the eyes of the law if I happened to hit one of them in the back. I switched my attention to the vehicle. I found that being unable to see the pistol made sighting difficult but, while I failed to produce the fireball that would have followed such action on the films or TV, I heard several metallic noises and one that sounded to me much like a bullet passing through toughened glass.

In retrospect, I can see that I had presented the enemy with an almost impossible choice – to stick around and face an armed madwoman or to brave the bullets which were plinking into their transport. When the magazine ran out, I paused to reload, which gave Ian his chance to grab the pistol out of my hands. Instinct must have urged the men to take the line of quickest departure. Snatching their opportunity, they ran for their vehicle.

My blood was up, too far up to be deterred by a husband who had been brainwashed by the law. These men had been after my blood and the blood of Bruce's father. They were running away and I was damned if they were coming back. I threw my weight against the door and fell out into the heather. The boot of the car had sprung open and I unbagged the first gun to hand, which turned out to be Ian's twelve-bore trap-gun. I had a mental picture of his cartridge belt rolled up in the corner of the boot. In three seconds, I had a pair of cartridges in my hand. By that time, the other vehicle was already in gear and tackling the steep hill, but I sent two loads of Number Six after it anyway and wished that I had thought to fill my pockets with BB. I doubt whether a single pellet overtook them, but the sound of the shots came echoing back from the hills and the flash lit the moor. At least they would be left in no doubt that we had heavier armament than a mere pistol and were not disinclined to use it.

The driver had got the message. He held his gear, in the interest of speed up the hill, until I thought that his engine would burst. And then he was over the first crest and round the shoulder of the hill and the noise was fading away.

We stood and breathed deeply. The moor, indeed the whole world, smelled sweet and fresh, of crushed bracken and heather and the water in the burn. A rabbit, disturbed by the noise, bolted suddenly past my feet and I heard crows overhead.

I reached into the car and put the lights on. That gave Ian the light that he needed to snatch his shotgun out of my hands. It was a measure of his concern that he put a dent in one barrel of his Remington with the butt of the Browning. 'What the hell were you playing at?' he shouted. 'You could have hurt somebody.'

That, I thought, was a bit thick; but Ian was not to blame. He was a dedicated policeman, and the criminal has always had more rights under the law than the victim. To the police, any member of the public who lifts a gun in self-defence is by definition a criminal. '*They* were trying to hurt *us*,' I said gently. 'Or hadn't you noticed?'

'You can't be sure of that,' he retorted. His voice had come down from alto to a mere tenor but it was still shaking.

'You sounded sure a couple of minutes ago.' My voice, I realized, was shaking too.

Wisely, he avoided that subject. 'Even if you didn't hit anybody, they could sue you for making holes in their truck.'

'I wish they would. That way, we'd be able to identify them. You didn't get their number?' Ian's silence was my answer. 'Nor did I,' I admitted.

We were both a little bit overwrought. We stood and continued with the deep breathing until we had calmed down a little. I found a peppermint in my pocket to help my dry mouth. I soothed Mac – who must have been wondering what sort of family he had adopted – and made sure that he was shut in the car before I groped in the boot for our big torch. The working parts of the car seemed to have suffered little serious damage. Ian wrenched some of the bodywork clear of the wheels and decided that it would probably be capable of motion. It was when we came to explore the route back to the road that we came across the weapon, presumably dropped by one of our attackers when he heard my bullets going past. It was a two-foot length of sycamore branch some three inches thick, reduced at one end to a comfortable thickness for the hand.

'A club?' I suggested. I gave an involuntary shiver but it was as much the chill of the breeze as the realization of what might have been. We were a long way north of home and higher up and the hour was late.

'Undoubtedly,' Ian said, abandoning all his disbelief.

'Rather crude.'

'Maybe,' Ian said, giving it a tentative swing. 'But a *coup de grâce* inflicted by this would have more chance of being passed off as the result of a car smash than knife-wounds or bullet-holes.'

Ian had come round to my way of thinking. There was no more mention of my shooting up the vicinity of Glen Dye. We set about considering the extraction of the car. We each kept one eye open in case of the return of my targets, but the next set of lights to approach came from the other direction and belonged to a lorry with a friendly driver who lent his weight alongside Ian's. With the two of them pushing – and calling out conflicting instructions – and me driving, we brought the car back to the road. The lorry driver was thanked. He refused any payment and went on his way, showing no curiosity. Apparently, accidents of that kind were not uncommon there.

I decided that I had driven enough for one lifetime, so perforce Ian took over again. The car sounded unhappy and handled, Ian said, like steering a cow by the tail, but it was transport. Mac the dog, more sad and confused than ever, squeezed between the seats and insisted on travelling sprawled across my lap. I was as glad of the comfort as he was.

Going cautiously, we went on our way, crossing the Dee at Potarch. It was late. Traffic had died and for most of the way there were no lights in sight. The route was confusing but Mr Munro's directions had been meticulous. Even so, midnight had come and long gone before we bumped up a rough farm road and stopped before a neat double-fronted house of the type known locally as one-and-a-half storeys, that is to say with rooms in the steep, slated roof and dormer windows protruding like frogs' eyes.

Yellow light spilled out of the front door and I saw the once familiar figure of Mr Munro, tall and lanky and now becoming stooped. I felt a rush of an affection that I had never realized was there.

Chapter Six

We were introduced to Mrs Jamieson, our hostess, who was as small and round as her brother was tall and skinny. Her silver hair was still thick but Mr Munro's few remaining hairs were brushed across his scalp. The sole similarity between the elderly siblings was the soft lilt of the Islands. Refreshments were offered, but each seemed relieved when we pleaded exhaustion and accepted only tea from the waiting pot. The hour was very late and they were early risers.

Before retiring to a neat bedroom under the sloping roof, however, we gave Mr Munro a brief account of our adventure on the Cairn o' Mount road, with one slight expurgation. Bearing in mind our host's strict views about firearms, Ian scaled down my barrage into a single shot fired into the air from my shotgun. Mr Munro seemed to feel that that much firepower, used purely as a deterrent, was regrettable but came just within the bounds of the permissible.

Mr Munro showed us to our room and made his own report in a low voice. His sister, it appeared, was not in his confidence. 'The telephone directory,' he told me, 'is of no help at all. Your man must be a tenant and the phone is unlisted and probably in somebody else's name.

Or yet another name of his own. Tomorrow, we can try the taxation office and the electoral register, but I am not hopeful. The man is too canny to be easily traced.'

I fought back a yawn and thanked him for trying.

As I lay beside Ian between the stiff white sheets, I could hear Mr Munro using the phone. He had been notable, I recalled, for his apparent lack of any need for sleep when there was work to be done. I hoped that he was making some arrangement about our car rather than reporting me to Grampian Police for the reckless discharge of a shotgun.

Moments later, I was in an exhausted sleep. I came out of it slowly, to realize that the sun was well up and Mr Munro, his eyes carefully averted both from my person and from my clothing on the chair, was putting a cup of tea on the bedside locker. 'Your husband is in the bathroom,' he said. 'I would have let you lie in, but callers are expected.'

He left me to wonder, in my still foggy mind, why I could not have been allowed to sleep until the callers had been and gone.

As I dragged myself out of the bed, assumed some sort of wakefulness and prepared to confront another damn day, I could hear hens below the window. From the window, the smallholding looked exceptionally tidy. Beyond the fruit trees and a field of barley, not yet ripe, I could see a dark wood of conifers and hills beyond, their lower slopes spattered with white dots which were sheep. Breakfast was porridge and more tea in a pleasantly old-fashioned kitchen, with home-baked bread and real butter to follow. Mac, who had slept on his cushion in the back door lobby, welcomed me as his only true friend in a harsh world. He seemed to expect food so I borrowed some meal and a dish from Mrs Jamieson's collie and gave him a small breakfast. Our car had already been collected by the local garage.

Ian and Mr Munro joined me at the breakfast table. Mrs Jamieson tactfully quitted the room. 'I've been ringing Newton Lauder,' Ian said. 'The only progress they've made at home, or all that I could get them to tell me over the phone, is that Foster's Volvo had agricultural diesel in the tank.'

Mr Munro tut-tutted. In his view, I remembered, an offence was an offence, be it serial murder or parking on a yellow line. 'The man was taking a risk,' he added. 'Cars are stopped and tested, hereabouts.'

'Those would be cars known to be diesel engined,' Ian said. 'The Volvo, on the surface, was a petrol model. And the car had been stolen anyway and the tax disc stolen and altered. If anybody looked twice at the car, he was probably quite prepared to walk away and leave it. Which, of course, is exactly what he did.'

I was nursing my second mug of tea. 'We should phone Mum and tell her that we've arrived more or less safely.'

'I've done that. You'll be pleased to hear that your father had a good night. You may also be pleased to hear that your insurers had phoned as soon as the regular staff came in this morning, to say that the customary reward would be offered for recovery of the guns.'

That made me prick my ears. The family has always had a rapprochement with insurance rewards; according to Dad, the purchase of Briesland House was largely funded by one. 'That should enable us to pay Mrs Jamieson for all the phone calls,' I suggested.

'We will not hear of it,' Mr Munro said indignantly.

Ian winked at me. 'In that case, will you make one more call? Phone the insurers about our car?'

'You do it,' I said. 'They'll go bananas if they hear my voice again.'

'It'll be different staff,' he said. 'You've only spoken to the weekend skeleton staff. And, after all, you were driving.'

'That's another reason,' I told him. 'They can't be nasty to you.'

He sighed theatrically. 'A husband's work is never done.'

'Yours never is,' I agreed.

'You see how she treats me?' he asked, apparently of Mr Munro. 'Beastess with the leastest! We've come all this way. When are you going to tell me what we do next? The ball seems to be in your court.'

'In point of fact,' I said, 'I've passed the ball to Mr Munro.'

'And I,' said Mr Munro, 'have passed it on. And if that is a car that I hear . . .' He went out, which saved him from having to continue the sporting metaphor. A few seconds later he returned. I noticed that he had to make a practised bob of the head to pass under the low lintel. 'There's somebody you must meet,' he said. 'Bring your tea with you and we'll sit out on the green. It's a bonny morn.'

He loaded three more mugs, the milk jug and the huge teapot onto a tray and bore them outside. We followed obediently. I brought Mac with me on a lead.

The 'green' was a small lawn behind the house where a neatly and strongly constructed wooden table and two benches stood in the precise, geometric centre of the grass. Round about, a fringe of bright flowers separated the lawn from rank upon rank of vegetables. The air was mild and warm and filled with the scent of the flowers.

The two men who were sitting there stood up to be introduced. The elder, and obviously the senior, was a man nearing Mr Munro's age, as tall and even leaner. His hair was grey, silvering at the temples but hardly thinning at all. He had a benevolent face, slightly marred by a nose once broken.

'Detective Inspector Fellowes and Mrs Fellowes,' Mr Munro said formally. 'This is Detective Chief Superintendent Goth. He and I were probationers together, many a year ago.'

'More years than I care to count,' Mr Goth said. 'How are you?' His voice had no more than a trace of the distinctive Aberdeenshire accent. I could hear a faint echo of Mr Foster in it. 'But I was fresh out of school while he had done his military service, so he was almost a father-figure to me. This is Detective Sergeant McIver.'

I was relieved when we sat down again because I was beginning to feel like a dwarf. DS McIver was almost as tall as the other two and about on a level with Ian. Like my husband, he was one of the freckled and sandy-haired Scotsmen. He had a pleasant smile, a dry hand and a firm grip. His voice was pure Highland, but not quite like Mr Munro's. Inverness, I guessed, and I later learned that I was right. Hearing the two together, the Hebridean and the mainland Highlander, I was struck again that people from areas where Gaelic was once the common language may differ slightly in accent but have in common a soft lilt and a precise use of the language which many an educated Englishman might envy.

'I know Mr James, your father's partner,' McIver said to me.

'We both do,' said Mr Goth. 'He gave us help on a case once.'

'But I have fished with him,' the DS said. Apparently that made a big difference. (I saw Ian's eyebrows begin to rise. From a lowly sergeant to a detective chief superintendent it was gross impertinence but Goth let it go. I guessed that McIver was privileged, perhaps being groomed for higher things.)

'I had heard of this racket the man was engaged in,' said Mr Goth. 'We had a scandal of our own, only last year. One of our officers, who was heading an anti-drugs operation, was found to be negotiating for a property that should have been far beyond his means. It seemed that he had found a rare and valuable book among the things that his father had left him. We had no real proof, but he was allowed to see that his career was going nowhere. He took an early retirement. So we take your experiences very seriously. When Hamish phoned yesterday, I called DS McIver in and asked him to see what he could do.'

'He knows about last night's incident?' Mr Munro asked.

Goth nodded. 'I'll leave the Sergeant with you. He will report to me direct. Officially, he will be conducting the investigation. If resources or backup are required, he has only to ask.'

'That is just what I had hoped for,' Mr Munro said. 'There are certain difficulties . . .'

'We understand what they might be,' Goth said. 'McIver?'

The DS nodded. 'I phoned Edinburgh this morning. The attitude was unhelpful, to say the least. In view of which, I gave them as little information about yourselves as I could.'

'Your father, Mrs Fellowes,' Goth said, 'may have trodden on our toes once or twice, but only by way of revealing the truth. Rather more often, he has proved helpful. It seems that our Edinburgh colleagues have taken that kind of help amiss.'

'That's so,' McIver said.

'At the moment,' said Goth, 'we only have a bald outline of the story. Tell it in detail.'

Between us, we went over the history, answering questions from all three men. When we seemed to be finished, Goth said, 'It seems clear except for the attack on you. Foster's best course would have been to drop out of sight and stay there. But no doubt his reasons will become clear.' He nodded to the sergeant.

McIver took a sip from his mug, opened a pocketbook and went on in his soft, Highland voice. 'There has not been much time, you understand, and most of that on a Sunday, but I will tell you what we have.

'After calling Edinburgh, I phoned Newton Lauder direct. They will be seeing what they can get from the Volvo, but they have no details yet except for the agricultural diesel oil in the tank. The descriptions given by your neighbours are conflicting and virtually useless; and no other witnesses have been found so far.

'As I told Mr Munro, McBean's Van Hire vans are blue. One of those vans was found deserted and burning near the Black Dog, just north of Aberdeen, at first light this morning. According to the firm, it had been hired by a gentleman who last month reported his driver's licence stolen along with other material in his wallet. He knows nothing of the matter and can account for his movements yesterday.

'Regarding the names Mr Munro obtained from the Falconry Society—'

'What?' said Ian.

'Did you not know?' McIver asked. 'I was wondering why you did not speak of it.'

'Speak of what?' Ian asked on a rising tone.

'Didn't I tell you about that?' I asked as casually as I could. I had quite forgotten to keep Ian informed about one of my leads.

'No you did not.'

'Please accept my apologies,' I said stiffly. The other three men were hiding smiles but Ian let it be seen that I had blotted my copybook. I decided to hurry on. 'Well, the first time that I looked at Mr Foster's car it was very clean, but I noticed a small feather in the driver's footwell. I couldn't say why, but its colour reminded me of the male peregrine that grabbed a wood pigeon and flew into the windscreen, that time that we went to Kelso.' (Ian nodded coldly.) 'Then Mrs Shaw, who has the antique shop at Coleburn, said that Foster was always after the big money items, but one exception that puzzled her was that once he bought a small bundle of leather straps, silver bells and a few feathers that had turned up in an old box. To me, that spelled falconry. So I tried the dog with the tinkle of a little bell and he lit up. He's been trained to work with hawks and falcons.'

'I have always said, since she was a child, that she was bright and observant,' Mr Munro said delightedly. 'But scatterbrained.'

Ian did a complete volte-face and rushed to my defence. 'After what she's coped with during the last twenty-four hours, it's no wonder that she missed explaining something to me.' Ian thought it over and decided to be gracious. 'That was clever. I take back what I said about needles and haystacks.'

McIver waited to be sure that we had finished our exchange. 'To that list,' he said, 'we added a few names of people who are not society members but have a licence from the Department of the Environment.'

'So quickly?' I said.

He shrugged. 'The impossible takes a little longer. I sent the D. of E. a fax last night and the reply came in before we set out this morning. I have asked local officers to check up discreetly – we do not want the man to bolt. I want to know whether any of those people resemble your description of Mr Foster or have a friend of that description – we must remember that Mr Foster himself may not be the falconer. I'll call in for the answers shortly.'

I had seen that Ian was uncertain what manner to adopt. He was off his territory and dealing with two officers, one junior and one much senior to him. Now he settled for being himself and came over better for it. 'Somebody should know him,' he said. 'But what if they don't? Or don't admit it?'

'We have a useful witness,' I said.

They each looked blank but Ian caught on first. 'Of

101

course!' he said. 'The dog! He'll know when he gets near home.'

'He'll know, all right,' I said. 'He may not want to let on. He seemed to settle down with me rather easily. Perhaps he wasn't happy with Mr Foster. I have a hunch that his over-polite and probably repressed master may have been one of those men who show affection to their dogs in public but take their tempers out on them afterwards.'

'We'll meet that problem when we come to it,' Ian said. 'Meantime, you'd better stop being so soft with him.'

'I am treating him with consideration,' I said. 'Is it my fault that the experience is new to him?'

'You are treating him as a pet, so yes.'

I maintained a dignified silence. There was a modicum of truth in what Ian said, but no more than a modicum – whatever that might be.

'The dog,' McIver said, 'would be the reason for the attack on yourselves. You returned to the house suddenly. Foster had to clear out quickly with his haul but there was a police car standing by his own vehicle. He could afford to lose the car, which he had stolen or which had been stolen to his order. And you may be right in supposing that he had no real affection for the dog. But he probably realized that the dog might lead us to his home. So he called on some hard men. They may be the ones who assisted at the robbery or another gang – he seems to be well connected in the criminal field. He could have whistled up a new team. They watched the house and followed you and made their attack at a propitious moment for recovering the dog and putting you out of action.'

'I take it,' Mr Munro said suddenly, 'that you were not followed here?'

'Definitely not,' Ian said, 'unless Foster can also whistle up a helicopter with a thermal imaging camera.'

'That's good. I am not afraid for myself, you understand, but I would not wish to put my sister into any danger.'

'I should think not,' Mr Goth said. 'We must move quickly, before he has time to get up to any more mischief. And also before he finds a way to move Mr Calder's guns. Go back to the car and see if we have any answers,' he told the Sergeant.

McIver closed his book with a snap and got to his feet. When the Sergeant was out of earshot, Mr Goth said, 'He's good, that boy. Some day he'll be very good. I had to bribe him away from Highland with his sergeant's stripes, but he'll be worth it in the long run. You'll be needing some official standing and maybe some backup. If I leave him with you for a few days—'

'We'll be very grateful,' Ian said.

'No call for gratitude. It's a proper use of resources. I want the lad to get experience of working on his own initiative. And we owe both Mr Calder and Mr James for help given in the past. Unlike our friends in the Lothians, we appreciate being put straight. Egg on our faces stopped worrying us long ago. You'll remember, Hamish . . .'

The two were lost in reminiscences, meaningless to me and only just comprehensible to Ian, until the Sergeant returned carrying a personal radio. He seated himself neatly and reopened his book. 'Nine reports so far,' he said. 'Three of them seem to be just possible.'

Mr Goth nodded and got to his feet. We walked with

him round the house. 'Check them out,' he told McIver. 'I'm leaving you to work with Inspector Fellowes. Keep me informed. I'll decide what to tell Edinburgh.'

'I'll be without a car,' McIver pointed out anxiously. 'Sir, perhaps I should come with you—'

'We will use my car,' Mr Munro said firmly.

Mr Goth grinned at him, lowered himself into the driver's seat of an unmarked Jaguar and fastened the seat belt. The Sergeant looked worried. 'I'll be all right,' Mr Goth told him. There was a gleam in his eye. I guessed that detective chief superintendents were usually chauffeured and did not often get an excuse to blast around in Jaguars at the public's expense. He took off in a burst of wheelspin that rattled gravel around us.

'You usually drive him in that car?' Mr Munro suggested.

McIver nodded. 'And I've treated it like my own, if not better.'

'That display may have been for your benefit.'

'I doubt it,' the Sergeant said. 'I think he's just enjoying himself. When he insisted on driving I sat beside him and clicked my tongue and tutted and hissed and trod on imaginary brakes. I did not mean to spoil his fun,' he added quickly. 'Mr Goth is not at all a bad driver. It is I who am a bad passenger. But somehow he never felt like driving again with me in the car.'

'I am not surprised in the least. We all need to get out of school from time to time. I am happy enough in my retirement,' Mr Munro said, 'but I shall be glad of a break from working the croft and decorating the wee house. Shall we go?'

Mr Munro drove. After all, it was his car. In most

respects he had always seemed to me to be cautious, hidebound, a do-it-by-the-book man. But when it came to driving, he was a different person. Perhaps, again, it was the police training. He had a Rover which I remembered from his later days in Newton Lauder, with a lot of miles on the clock but impeccably maintained, and he managed to burn up the road without ever getting a squeal from the tyres or a complaint from his passengers. After a few tense seconds I could see Ian and even the DS relaxing.

DS McIver had the front passenger seat, by virtue of the fact that he knew where we were going. Ian and I took up the rear and I had Mac again sprawled across my knees – a position which he seemed to be coming to expect and appreciate. From time to time, he nosed my hand as though seeking reassurance.

Before we had gone ten miles, Detective Sergeant McIver was asking us to call him Tony. I decided that his friendly and informal disposition would get him into trouble one of these days. Ex-Chief Superintendent Munro agreed immediately but without reciprocating. Ian's rank was still new to him so that familiarity with a mere sergeant – his own rank six months earlier – went against the grain, but in the end they were Tony and Ian.

'I'm Deborah,' I said. Nobody had asked.

From what Tony said – and, looking over his shoulder, by my reading of the map – several of the falconers (and, to be pedantic, austringers, as those who keep and fly hawks rather than falcons are properly called) lived as far apart as Inverness, Aviemore and Montrose but, by good fortune, the three most likely candidates were all to be found in Aberdeenshire.

Raptors require space for training and exercise, so

each lived in or close to open country. The first had a post-war bungalow with well-kept outbuildings. It was built of almost convincing artificial stone, but the tall and comparatively narrow windows traditionally dictated by the limitations of stone lintels had been replaced by picture windows, so that the house had an unlikely look and seemed to be in danger of collapse. It was set back from a secondary road behind a rigidly disciplined garden. Ian brought the car to rest.

Tony McIver glanced over his shoulder and saw that Mac was looking out of the window without displaying the least interest. He looked at his notes. 'Our witness isn't in a hurry to make an identification. I'll start this one off alone,' he said. 'The description fits and he's said to be very polite, but he's holding down a job. He'll be at work but his wife's at home. I can see movement. If I think that he's a possible, I'll fix it so that Mrs Fellowes – Deborah – gets a look at him. For the moment, I think my story is that I'm on a routine visit, looking for a missing person.'

He followed a serpentine path between the flower beds, rang the doorbell and showed his identification to an invisible presence who answered the door. He disappeared. We waited. I had not expected Mr Foster to be married, nor to have a regular job. With what we knew of him, marriage was unlikely and full-time employment almost impossible. The whole exercise was beginning to look like a terrible exercise in futility.

Tony came out. He lingered on the doorstep for a parting word with a stout brunette in her forties and then came back to the car. 'Straight on,' he said, 'and left at the main road.'

'I take it that that was not *chez* Foster,' said Ian.

'The lady showed me photographs of her husband,' Tony said. 'The general appearance is much the same, assuming that your Videofit is a good match, but there it ends. For one thing alone, you mentioned that Mr Foster had small feet.'

'Dad noticed it too,' I said.

'She laughed when I asked to see his shoes. "Like something out of Agatha Christie," she said. To judge from his shoes, he should be one of us. Elevens, at least. If he is as stocky as you have made him out to be, he must look a bit like Donald Duck.'

I happened to know that both Ian and Mr Munro were sensitive to jokes about policemen's feet. I jumped in before acrimony could develop. 'I hope that you didn't say so,' I told him. 'Did she recognize the Videofit?'

'I showed it to her. She thought that she might have seen the man on some occasion when a number of falconers met to fly their birds at grouse – by kind permission, she said, of Sir Horace McBeth. But he did not have birds of his own and she could not remember who he arrived with. She said that his dog – this dog, I hope,' Tony said, twisting again to look down at Mac, who twitched his tail placatingly, 'seemed to have had experience at working to falcons.' (I began to feel hopeful again. Even Mac, on my knee, seemed to stir.) 'I wanted to bring her out to meet the dog, but she said that she couldn't possibly tell one dog from another, especially after an interval of six months. She said that all dogs look alike to her.'

'Ridiculous!' I said as the car moved off again. To me all dogs are individual, even more so than people. Dogs, after all, have variety of colour and markings not to be seen in humans.

Tony was poring over his map. 'The next two live within a mile of each other,' he said, 'either side of a village. Neither man is anything like your Videofit. They're noted as possibilities only because a blue Volvo estate has been seen in the village from time to time and the local bobby has several times seen a man matching Mr Foster's description buying a paper in the village shop.'

The countryside was looking its best. We were passing the only eyesore, a burned-out garage and filling station, when a call came in on Tony's radio. I could hear the quacking from his speaker but, being unpractised at the art of interpreting speech largely deficient in consonants, could hardly make out a word of it. 'Two more reports but only one of them seems hopeful. Oh, the devil!' Tony exclaimed, poking a finger at the map. 'We must have passed it. Well, we can call there on the way back.'

Mac showed no interest in our next two customers. One was a retired designer living in a converted barn; the other's wife redirected us to the garage in the village which her husband owned and ran. Tony saw both men and satisfied himself that neither of them either was or knew Mr Foster.

'We'll go back by the way we came,' he told Mr Munro. 'If this doesn't bear fruit, we'll have to try the less likely prospects while we wait for some more reports. And travel further afield.'

'Och well,' Mr Munro replied philosophically, 'it is a fine morning for a drive in the countryside.'

The last of our possibles lived in a farmhouse, set

back from the road behind a recently planted orchard. He was, said Tony, a game dealer working out of the former farm outbuildings. He was single and described as 'contermacious' by the local sergeant.

As Mr Munro brought the car to a halt beside the road, I could read a sign on the gable – 'G. Carmichael, Game and Venison', with a phone number. A more modest sign on the gate informed us that the name of the house was Kilcreggan.

Mac stirred on my knee – as, I realized, he had done when we passed the place earlier. 'We have a reaction,' I said.

'Not a very happy reaction,' Mr Munro commented.

'What do you expect,' I retorted, 'with the three of you all craning round to glare at the poor dog?' But Mac was not keen to get out of the car and the vibrations that I could feel through my knees were of apprehension. He had been here before, but the place did not hold the best of memories. I ran my fingers through his soft hair, smoothing down the hackles. 'Also,' I added, 'I suspect that Mr Foster is one of those dog trainers who would just as soon be obeyed out of fear as out of the dog's eagerness to please.'

'From the description,' Tony said, 'the Gordon Carmichael who lives here is as unlike your Mr Foster as you can get. Now, he may be his non-identical twin brother or only a casual acquaintance. Am I doing it right? Shall I continue to soft-pedal and try to suggest that it's a matter not important enough to be worth protecting his pal? Or do we go in with guns blazing in the hope of blasting an immediate answer out of him? Either way, if we get it wrong we could get it *very* wrong.'

109

'You are the local boy,' Mr Munro said. 'It's your decision.'

'But I'm only a poor, misbegotten detective sergeant,' Tony McIver said plaintively. 'You're a detective inspector, for God's sake, and a former chief superintendent. I'm used to being told what to do. So tell me.'

'I rather think,' Mr Munro said, 'that Mr Goth may have thrown you in at the deep end to see whether you can swim. He wants to know whether you are promotion material or if he is wasting his time and patronage.'

'I see,' Tony said slowly. 'And he'll ask you later for a report on how I got on?'

'In his shoes, it is what I would do.'

I could have pointed out that Chief Superintendent Goth might not be as much of a devious bastard as Mr Munro had been, but I remained silent. Tony McIver's guess had as good a chance of being right as anyone else's.

Ian, however, took pity. 'I always believe that the acid test of staff is the ability to seek and take advice, so here's mine, for what little it's worth. Start gently, watch him and if his behaviour or your instinct tells you that he's hiding something, put the boot in. Or come out and we'll try the dog.'

Tony McIver nodded gratefully. 'Very well. If we had the whole of the Regional Crime Squad with us we would still not have any evidence to confront him with, except for the testimony of a dog – and a mongrel dog at that! I shall try the softly-softly approach first. If that fails, we may have to see what a little hectoring can do.'

He left the car where it was, shaded and half hidden by a full-grown beech. I continued soothing the dog while

I looked out at the countryside. The patchwork of fields and small woods looked very much like any comparable scene at home although the air was noticeably cooler and the cereal crops were not quite so advanced. Half a mile away I could see farm buildings, with new barns and large silos. During the boom years, now past, one farm had swallowed one or more others, forcing vacated farmhouses onto the open market. Mr Carmichael presumably occupied one of them.

'He's taking his time,' Ian said at last.

'Perhaps no news is good news,' Mr Munro said. He sounded unconvinced.

'Shall I try the dog?' I asked.

'Hold your horses,' said Ian. 'Hold your dog, rather. Here he comes.'

Tony McIver was looking angry. He stamped down the path and threw himself into the passenger seat. 'He denies all knowledge of anybody resembling the Videofit under any of the names we've got. I think he's lying but I can't be sure.'

'I was just going to try the dog,' I told him.

'I was just going to suggest it.'

'He's been here before,' I said, 'but, of course, he may only have come by car. It's worth a try.'

'So try,' Tony said. 'We'll follow in the car. And I'll get on the radio to tell the locals to come and watch the place.'

I opened my door and coaxed a reluctant Mac out onto the verge. While I put a lead on him, his tail was down and he kept his face away from the house. I sensed that he trusted me and however inconsiderately he had been treated, home, I told myself, would still be home. I hoped that I had not spoiled the homing instinct out of him. The word *home* seemed to have no very favourable meaning for him, but after sniffing around the verge for a few seconds he set off slowly along the roadside. Keeping a slack lead, I followed. He looked back and up at me several times, seeming reassured by my company. In fits and starts, the car followed us.

After what must have been half a mile, Mac crossed the road and we took to a narrow but tarred farm-road between fields of barley. He increased his pace as if heading for his accustomed source of shelter and food and I had to hurry if I was to keep the lead slack rather than suggest a different direction to him.

The farm-road forked. Mac trotted to the left, pausing only to mark his territory. A sign on the fence announced that the way led to Mowdiemoss. We were descending into a shallow valley where trees hung over a stream. I thought that I could hear a vehicle in motion somewhere ahead, but the sound died away. We were approaching a cluster of small farm buildings. The tidiness and the lack of agricultural smells suggested that this was another farmhouse which had been put on the open market when the land was taken over, but I thought that I could detect a faint trace of freshly burned exhaust hanging on the calm air.

Mac came to a halt in a yard between the house and an L-shaped row of granite and slate outbuildings. There were tall trees around and water not far away so that the place was attractively cool and the stones were mossy. In winter, I thought, it would be rather less cosy. With a sudden jolt, I noticed the carriage lamp over the house door and realized that I had rushed in where others might have feared to tread. But the place had a deserted feel to it and I was still sure that a vehicle had only just driven off. Mac looked towards an open-fronted shed. I let him off the lead and he went inside and lay down on a pile of dry and clean-looking sacks, curling unhappily. This, I assumed, was his usual bed.

The car stopped in the mouth of the yard and the three men got out. Tony McIver, the only one with any pretence to an official position locally, walked to the door and knocked loudly.

They were looking for a cog in the wheels of corruption. I was more concerned with whether Dad's guns were on the premises. I went to the nearest doorway. The double doors were standing open. The space seemed to have been used as a garage but no car was there now.

Tony was not getting any answer at the house. I heard him say, 'It's not locked.'

'I think he's made tracks,' I said.

'Dash it!' Tony said. 'If you're right . . . I wonder how much cooperation I can call on.'

The open-fronted cart shed was obviously bare except for a few gardening tools. Beyond was another pair of doors. I pulled one open. The long shed had probably begun as a feed store. It seemed empty now except for a few packing cases, just as empty. They might once have held the guns but I thought not. The sizes looked wrong. I turned to go but my eye was caught by what seemed to be a bundle of cloth half hidden by one of the packing cases. Hoping that I might have found at least the cloths that Mr Foster had used as packing material, I took a closer look.

After a second, I realized that I was looking at the

body of a man. He was as dead as a man can be; and recently dead – the blood on his shirt was still bright and wet. He had been stabbed several times through the neck and body and the knife was still in his chest. I recognized the ornate silver-mounted handle of my father's kris.

Chapter Seven

Stay cool, I told myself, and *Think*, and *Try to do whatever Dad would have done.* Too much might depend on the next few minutes. I stole time for a quick glance out of the door. The others were still gathered by the door of the house, arguing over whether it would be permissible to go inside. I had time to scan the body and its surroundings. It was not the first body that I had seen, but nearly so. It was very still but somehow that made the sight more bearable. If it had twitched, I would have bolted.

Then I withdrew to the point nearest the door from which the body could be seen and I uttered the sort of noise that I guessed a self-contained lady might produce when confronted by an unexpected corpse. It needed no effort.

The others came running. Tony took one look and snapped, 'Everybody outside!' Others might outrank him, but he was local and so he had authority. We filed outside and waited until he emerged.

'Did you touch anything?' he asked me.

'Just the doorhandle.'

He studied the handle, a cast-iron ring powdered with rust. 'And if that would take a fingerprint, I'll eat it.' He paused and thought furiously, then used his radio to send a message to be relayed to the local bobby, telling him, without explanation, to follow us up.

'We only have a few minutes,' he pointed out to us, 'so we must decide quickly. This is the way of it. You know as well as I do how these things go. The first officer on the scene will be required to stick around, preserving the evidence. Then, so that when the case comes to court "best evidence" can be presented, he becomes the muggins who has to take over the accepting of every scrap of evidence, registering, sealing, storage, delivery to Forensic, collection, production and attestation in court.' (Ian and Mr Munro were nodding solemnly.) 'Well,' Tony resumed, 'any dimwit can attend to all that. On the other hand, we have an interesting inquiry on our hands which is bound to represent part if not all of the bigger crime. If I report the body, I'll be stuck with the administrative details. I think we can be more use moving quickly to follow our present leads.

'So I propose to let the local lad find the body. It could be a good career move for him and it will leave me free to chase your guns and therefore at the same time chase the probable murderer. But I can only do that if I have your solemn promises never, under any circumstances, to let on that I saw the body first.'

'You can have my word,' Ian said. I just nodded.

Mr Munro pursed his lips, which gave him the look of a sulky camel. 'That would be very irregular,' he said.

Tony McIver shrugged. 'In that case, you'll have to manage without me. Or perhaps you'll give us your help on the murder? The big guns from the Borders with some special knowledge of the background . . . The solution to

116

tho murder may also be the solution to where Mr Calder's guns have gone.' *And it may not*, he might have added.

Our chances of success would be reduced almost to nil without Tony and the support he could call on from Grampian Police and the rest of the Scottish forces. I adopted my most wheedling tone and tried to recreate the look of the little girl whom Mr Munro had formerly dandled on his knee. 'The two cases are really the same,' I said. 'Catch Mr Foster and you've caught the murderer. Well, we're trying to catch him, but if Tony has to waste time trying to convince his superiors that he would be more use working with us than following up dull routine, then Mr Foster will be away and gone before we can take up the chase. In all honesty, would Tony be doing more good chasing Mr Foster and the guns with us or getting bogged down in statements and . . . and . . . ?'

I petered out. I had a mental picture of hanging round incident rooms, waiting to give more and more useless statements. That was as far as my experience of police routines would stretch. But Mr Munro caught my drift, or else he was swayed by my obvious anxiety. 'It is, as I said, irregular. But the girl has a point,' he said reluctantly, 'a definite point. And I am no longer a serving officer. Very well. I will connive. You have my promise.'

'Very well,' Tony echoed. 'With the possible exception of something which we have already forgotten, bear witness that I am telling nothing but the truth.'

He made radio contact with his headquarters and began a discussion with Chief Superintendent Goth, relayed through at least one other officer, but I slipped away. There was something I wanted urgently to know. The door of the house was standing ajar. I sidled through.

In the small hall, doors to a sitting room, a kitchen and a bedroom stood wide open and I could see a jumble of odds and ends tumbled about the rooms. I was ready to guess that Mr Foster had hurriedly packed up anything valuable or informative before heading for pastures new, abandoning the debris of his life for those who came after to interpret.

In the hall, a modern telephone hung on the wall. I could not imagine any fingerprints on it having any value in evidence but I lifted the receiver using a piece of paper from my handbag and I dialled 1471 with the blunt end of my pen. A recorded female voice gave me the number of the last caller. While the voice was still speaking, I realized my mistake. As a belated afterthought I did what I should have done first and keyed for Last Number Redial. All that I achieved was to reach 1471 again. A bad mistake! The others, I decided, must never know.

Tony had finished his confabulation. He saw me slip out of the house and he looked scandalized 'What were you doing in there?' he demanded. 'Did you touch anything?'

'I haven't ruined any of your precious clues,' I told him, hoping that it was true.

He took my statement at face value. 'Do we know who the corpse is?' he asked the world in general.

That piece of information was all that I had gained from my brief study of the murder scene. 'Mr Foster had some sort of dealings with a Toby Douglas,' I said. 'Mrs Shaw described him to me as small, wrinkled, bald and rat-faced. I don't want to speak ill of the dead but, from what little I saw of the body, the cap could fit. She said

118

that he deals from a store in Falkirk or Grangemouth or somewhere round about – she didn't seem at all sure.'

Tony McIver nodded and jotted the information down. 'With a bit of luck, he'll have identification on him. Otherwise, I'll have to ask for a description of the body and then pass that titbit on as coming from you.'

A small blue and white panda car was bouncing along the track. Tony hustled us back into the car. I whistled for Mac and he came out of the shed with a rush and fairly hurled himself into the car and on top of me, grinning as dogs can grin. Ian and Mr Munro looked at me sideways but made no protest. I was prepared to refuse flatly to leave Mac in the care of the police machine.

Tony walked to meet the local uniformed bobby and showed his identification. 'You know that we're looking for the man in the Videofit?' he asked.

The young man nodded and patted his tunic. 'I've a print of it in my pocket.'

'Good. We think he was living here. In particular, we're on the lookout for stolen property in the form of antique firearms. So take a good look around and don't miss the outbuildings. If anybody turns up, hang onto them. You can reach me by radio.'

The bobby touched his peak. 'Right you are, Sarge.'

Tony hopped into the car and nodded to Mr Munro. 'Back to Mr Carmichael's house,' he said. 'And a little haste might pay dividends.'

Mr Munro had not forgotten his old skills and I think that there was a touch of nostalgic pleasure in being called upon to make use of them. He took the farm-road at a speed which ironed out the ruts and potholes.

Tony McIver twisted his neck to look back at me. 'Do

you do shorthand?' he asked me through clenched teeth. As he had told us, he was not a relaxed passenger.

'Of a sort,' I told him. 'I started to learn it at one time but gave up. Now I have a system of my own that sort of grew out of what I could remember of the Pitman.'

He handed me his notebook. 'Good. I wouldn't want to leave you alone in the car with villains on the loose. This way you can pass for a WPC.'

I had had no intention of being left in the car so I accepted the notebook and tried to recall the demeanour of such WPCs as I had seen or met.

Mr Munro drew up outside Kilcreggan. The phone number on the signboard, I noted, agreed with the number quoted by the electronic voice. It seemed certain that Mr Carmichael had telephoned a warning. Mr Carmichael, I decided, was going to suffer, even if I had to come back after the others had gone and jump up and down on him in stiletto heels.

I pushed Mac off my knee and told him to sit and wait in the car. He complied with every sign of being too contented to object. It seemed that he was contemplating new ownership with relief.

Tony was ahead of us up the path and beating a tattoo with a polished brass knocker in the form of a stag's head. The door was opened by a man who struck me as being the stereotype Scotsman as might be envisaged by a lady at the court of Queen Victoria. He was large in all directions, with curly red hair and a beard to match, both of them in need of a trim, and he wore a kilt of Hunting McHaggis tartan complete with badger-mask sporran and *sgian dubh*.

Tony, who had seen the display before and, moreover,

came from an area where the kilt is everyday attire, remained unimpressed. 'Mr Carmichael,' he said formally, 'I have already introduced myself to you as Detective Sergeant McIver. I am now accompanied by Detective Inspector Fellowes and ex-Chief Superintendent Munro. May we come in?' The *ex-* was only audible because I was listening for it and there was no mention of Ian being a long way off his proper territory.

'And if I say no?'

'Then we will discuss what we have to discuss here, for the entertainment of your staff and any passers-by, and if we are not satisfied with our discussion it will be continued on police premises. And it may be that you will have health inspectors on your doorstep two days out of three from now on.' There was a new snap to his voice. This was a new Tony McIver to us and one with whom I would not have cared to argue.

Carmichael hesitated but the swish of a hose from an outbuilding helped him to make up his mind. With a poor grace he stepped aside and held the door. Tony led us, apparently by homing instinct, into a large sitting room which had been created by throwing together two rooms of the old house. The furniture and decor were contemporary but somehow unrelated, as though the selections had been made from different pages of one of the minor home-making magazines. There was no inspired rule-breaking, just a too well-ordered harmony of colour and materials extending even to the few flowers. There was the hand of a woman here, I decided, but not a very creative one. Even so, it would have been a relaxed room but for its owner's obvious frustration and bad temper.

The three policemen (two serving and one retired)

took seats. I sat at a table in the window where I could rest Tony's notebook and still observe the proceedings. Carmichael took a stand on the hearthrug, but when he realized that his position, instead of giving him dominance, reflected that of a subordinate on the carpet, he dumped himself into a corner of the settee.

'So what's it all about?' he growled.

Tony paused. I looked up in time to see him glance at Ian and I realized suddenly what was in his mind. It might look very peculiar to Mr Carmichael if a mere sergeant were to conduct an interrogation in the presence of two more senior officers. Ian, caught on the hop, dithered for a moment. 'You don't know?' he asked, buying a little time.

'No, I don't bloody well know.' If I had not already been sure that he was lying, the bluster in his voice would have given him away.

Ian had collected his thoughts. 'But you knew that we were interested in the man at Mowdiemoss? The Sergeant showed you the Videofit.'

Carmichael laughed harshly. 'Whoever recognizes a Videofit?'

'This happens to be a particularly good likeness which has been recognized by everyone else who has seen it and who has ever set eyes on the man,' Ian said with pardonable exaggeration. I sent him an urgent telepathic message. Either the message arrived safely or he was thinking along a parallel track. 'And so did you. You telephoned him as soon as the Sergeant's back was turned. He has now done a runner.'

'I deny it absolutely.'

My shorthand was coming back to me and I could

now spare enough attention to take part. Rather than admit to having tampered with the evidence I asked, 'Shall I try the Last Number Redial facility?'

Tony, who was nearest to Mr Carmichael's telephone, put out a hand.

Mr Carmichael took his eyes off my legs and gave my face a passing glare. 'All right,' he said furiously. 'All bloody right! So I phoned a friend. There's no law against it.' Evidently he had not even tried to cover his tracks, either by keying 141 before making the call nor by making another call afterwards. My opinion of his intelligence sank through the floor.

'No,' Ian said mildly. 'There's no law against phoning a friend. So he *is* a friend? A good friend?'

'I know him.'

'By what name?' Ian asked.

'What the hell is that supposed to mean?'

'I'll explain. The man in the Videofit was known to us by the name of Foster. He has also gone by the name of Julian Edwards and several others. By what name or names did you know him?'

Carmichael came suddenly off the boil and sat motionless.

'Well?' Ian said.

The radio in Tony's pocket chose that moment to start making noises. He tried it but it only crackled and buzzed.

'Take it outside, Sergeant,' Mr Munro said comfortably. Tony rose and went out.

'Well?' Ian repeated.

Carmichael had had time to think. He pulled himself together. 'First, I think that you should tell me what this is about.'

123

'I have no objection,' Ian said. 'Originally it was about fraud and corruption. More recently, theft on a grand scale. Also conspiracy to commit assault. What name was he known by locally? Come on, man,' he added. 'There must be others around here who knew him by one name or another. You can't do your good friend a favour by trying to keep his name from us. You can only delay us – and make us wonder how close you both were.'

'I knew him as Banks,' Carmichael said sullenly. 'Ewan Banks. But I knew nothing of any of this. And he wasn't a friend. I hardly knew him. He was just a nodding acquaintance.'

Mr Munro stirred. 'A nodding acquaintance,' he said softly, 'who trained his dog to work to your falcons and who you telephoned immediately after you were visited, to warn him that the police were asking questions. It seems to us that you must have trusted him absolutely. Or else you were closely associated. And now you are answering questions about as eagerly as you would visit the dentist. What vehicle would Mr Banks have been driving?' He looked up as Tony appeared in the doorway.

Mr Carmichael's red hair seemed to bristle in all directions. I thought that he was on the point of leaping to his feet and snatching down from above the fireplace one of the crossed claymores – repros, I noticed, from Forfarmetals. But he restrained himself and only grunted, 'I have no more to say except in the presence of my solicitor.'

'That is your privilege,' Tony said, 'and on most occasions it would be the wisest course. This time, however, I think that you would be making a serious mistake.' He came into the room. He was standing over Carmichael but he was looking at Ian 'That message was to tell us that the body of a man, apparently stabbed to death, has been found in an outbuilding at Mowdiemoss. He appears to have died of stab wounds, and within the last hour or two. We are more than ever anxious to interview Mr Banks.'

Each of us managed to produce at least a gasp of astonishment. I had a feeling that there was a degree of overacting but Carmichael seemed not to notice.

Ian took up the running again. 'At the moment, and according to your own story, you have done nothing worse than to phone a friend. You know whether that story is the truth. As you said, there is no law against phoning a friend – I do it all the time. But there is a law against warning a murderer that the police are coming to collect him. What happens to you may well depend on which version we come to believe.

'If you refuse to cooperate, you could hamper our inquiries seriously. For all we know, you may be waiting for a chance to render Mr Banks more aid than you already have. So, as long as we believe that you are holding back any information, however trivial, we cannot leave you at liberty. We will have no alternative but to take you in custody on suspicion of being an accessory.'

A silence gave me time to look at Carmichael. From being a film-maker's image of a Highlander at the height of the '45 rebellion, he was suddenly a very worried game dealer in fancy dress. 'Who's dead?' he asked.

'He is described as small, sharp-featured, bald and very wrinkled,' Ian said. 'Who would that be?'

'I . . . he sounds like a man who came looking for Ewan – Mr Banks – once. I've no idea who he was. Really.

What do you want to know?' Carmichael's accent, which had been barely perceptible, was stronger and definitely local.

'We have his car,' Ian said. 'The Volvo. But he and his associates hired a van yesterday in order to commit a robbery in the Borders. Do you deny being with them?'

'Of course I do.' Carmichael's voice had gone up towards a squeak. His hair still stood up, but defensively, with fear. It no longer bristled.

'Of course, you'd have to. We shall see,' Ian said grimly. 'The van has been found burning. But later last night his associates, with or without Banks himself, were using another substantial vehicle, something like an estate car but very big, with which they attempted to waylay a witness on the Cairn o' Mount road. Did they take you along on that trip?'

'God's sake, no,' Carmichael insisted shrilly.

'Banks may be escaping in that vehicle. He may commit further crimes. We need a description of it. If you could give us such a description and don't, you can imagine for yourself just how deep is the trouble you're in.'

There was a brief silence. I thought that Ian might have pitched it a little strong, but Carmichael swallowed it whole. 'I knew nothing of any of this,' he pleaded. 'Nothing at all. If I was guilty of anything I wouldn't be here and admitting this, I'd be running instead.' He forced an uneasy smile. 'But that may have been my car. Ewan – Mr Banks – turned up here yesterday evening, around six. He said that he'd had a breakdown in his Volvo and he needed the loan of my car, to move some antique furniture.'

'And you don't have it back yet?'

Carmichael shook his head miserably.

'I doubt you ever will,' Mr Munro put in. 'So you were friendly enough with him to lend him a car?'

'Just about.'

'Describe the car.'

'It's a GML Sierra Classic.'

'That's a specification, not a description,' Tony said. 'I don't suppose one officer in a thousand would know what one of those looks like.'

Carmichael hurried to make good the deficiency. 'It's much what the Inspector said. It's a very big estate car – I need something with a capacity to carry a load when it's needed. American built, of course, but right-hand drive. Dark red colour. And it's fitted with a black nudge bar – you know? – what they've started calling a bull bar.'

'Registration number?'

Carmichael quoted the number and Tony went outside to relay the fresh information.

The delay gave me time to think and Tony's use of the radio supplied the connection. It had seemed to me that Mr Foster (alias Edwards alias Banks) had been on an impossibly tight schedule. Then I remembered. 'He has a mobile phone, hasn't he?' I asked.

Carmichael looked at me in surprise. Until then I had been a faceless minion. 'As a matter of fact, he does. I noticed him fidgeting with it while he was asking me about the car.'

I wrote down the question and answer while congratulating myself on resolving one tiny corner of the mystery. The timetable made sense if Mr Foster – et cetera – had remained in touch with somebody whom he had left to keep an eye on us. Somebody, perhaps, on a motorcycle. I had seen a smart BMW motorbike in my mirror several times while I was driving north and that bike or its twin had taken on petrol at Stracathro.

Tony returned and resumed his seat. 'There was a message for you,' he told Ian. 'They found agricultural diesel in the tank of the Volvo. Where would he have got that?'

'Not around here,' Carmichael said. 'The local police are tigers on cheating the Customs and Excise, and the farmers around here take it seriously.'

Ian nodded. 'All units will be watching out for your vehicle,' he said. 'They're being warned that he may be dangerous. He'll be spotted if he sticks to the major roads. Where will he be heading?' he asked the now miserable Carmichael.

'Don't know.'

I thought that there was a return of the old truculence but Ian dealt with it in short time. 'You'd better know,' he said firmly. 'If it turns out that you could have helped but didn't, that you bought time for him to get away or even to kill again, you'll be the sorriest man in Scotland. I guarantee it, personally, and in that department my track record is unequalled.'

Carmichael was sweating. 'I honest to God don't know. He told me nothing. Why would he?'

Mr Munro leaned forward. 'It is my experience that everyone knows more than he knows he knows. So let us just find out how much you do know. When did your good friend Mr Banks first arrive at Mowdiemoss?'

'He's not . . .' Carmichael caught Mr Munro's eye and broke off. He swallowed. 'He's lived here longer than I

128

have. I bought this place eight years back and he was there already.'

'And how did you get to be so friendly with him?'

Again I thought that Carmichael was going to protest, but he must have realized in time that Mr Munro was only needling him. 'I got permission to fly my falcons over three or four farms. He saw me and he was hooked. So when one of the local farm dogs had an unplanned litter he took on a pup and we trained him to work to the falcons. He – Banks – came out with me, during the season, whenever he was at home.'

'And how much time did he spend away from home?'

Carmichael gave it some thought. 'I wasn't making notes, but I suppose he went away on business for about a week at a time, maybe once or twice a month, sometimes less.' He paused again and gathered courage for a question of his own. 'What was he really up to?'

Ian regarded him stonily. 'Again, I don't mind answering that because it leads into my next question. Your friend was involved in a racket involving antiques, but it's gone far beyond that now. Did he ever store any antiques with you?'

'Definitely not. Why would he need my space?' Carmichael asked reasonably.

'Or packing cases? In your cold store, perhaps?'

Carmichael shook his head. 'I need all the space I've got here, but he had more storage than he could ever fill at Mowdiemoss.'

'Did you ever see him handling any·goods? Or see what he had in store?'

The game dealer shook his red head again.

Ian changed tack. 'What can you tell us about the dead man, assuming him to be the man who came looking for your friend!'

Carmichael shrugged helplessly. 'I'd help if I could, but I've told you all I know.'

'He's said to have been on the fringe of the antique trade. Known – to us at least – as Toby Douglas. Small, bald, wrinkled and rat-faced. Come on, now. Doesn't that ring any bells?'

Carmichael tried on a smile for size but it was a poor fit. 'I could say that half the antique dealers I've met have fitted that description. What can I add? He turned up at Mowdiemoss one day. I was only there to pick Banks up to go to a meeting of falconers near Oldmeldrum. Ewan Banks didn't look too suited that I'd seen him. Ewan didn't introduce him and seemed damned careful to give nothing away in front of me but, come to think of it, I believe I heard him call the man *Mr Douglas*.'

There was a pause. Tony McIver took up the running again, but feeling his way. 'What did you think of the man known to you as Ewan Banks?'

Carmichael shrugged. 'We get – got – along all right. I made sure of that.'

Tony sat up straighter. I think that we all stirred. 'Why was that?' Tony asked.

The red beard curled in on itself as Carmichael made a face. 'He's very polite. On the surface, the politest man you'll ever meet. He's considerate and patient, so much so that it was a moon before I jaloused that there's another man beneath. A bad man to cross. A man who was suppressing a . . . a cauldron of temper. Or you might say, sitting on the safety valve. And more.'

'More?'

'Aye.' Carmichael was scowling furiously but I judged that it was only due to the effort of verbalizing his intuitions while overcoming his dread of the man. His accent and his dialect were slipping. 'He liked fine to come out with the birds,' he said at last. 'My falcons. We'd have been out there daily if he'd had his way. But after a while I jaloused that he took little pleasure in what pleased me, the soaring flight, the beauty of the stoop, the fierce arrogance of the birds.' For a moment, he was human and almost likeable as his pleasure shone through. Then he scowled again. 'Banks got a kick from watching the kill. He savoured it. It was as if he fed on the fear, the pain and the death of the quarry. Not the sort of a man falconers want among them, but I couldn't tell him that.' Carmichael shook his head. 'He went hare coursing when he could. It's no more than a guess – he knew fine I'd not go along with him – but my guess is that he used to follow less legal sports. Dogfighting. Badger baiting. The like of that.'

'Did he shoot?' I asked, remembering Mr Foster's comparative ignorance about guns.

Carmichael focused on me again. I used the interval to drop the pen and stretch my aching fingers. 'He'd have liked it,' Carmichael said at last. 'He tried. But he was no damn good at it, not with a shotgun. He's badly coordinated and he has a serious master-eye problem. I could have cured him of that, but by then I kent that he was not the sort of man to be let loose with a gun.'

Left to myself I would have been tempted to follow up the boast that he could cure master-eye problems. Ian, quite rightly, was not to be diverted. 'Let's get back to his character,' he said impatiently. 'Is there a special woman in his life?'

I looked up again in time to catch a glance from Carmichael. 'Dozens,' he said, 'but not one of them special. He enjoys women but he never sticks with one. The next is aye just around the corner. Damned if I know how he does it. That sleekit charm can work it every time.' There was a trace of envy in his voice.

'Given that he has a temper,' Ian said, 'or even that he has a sadistic streak, why does that make him a bad man to cross?'

'It's just the way he is. He aye has to win, canna thole losing. He holds wide of argie-bargie in public, but . . . Here's just one instance. He had the de'il of a stramash with the local garage. He was certain sure they'd over-charged him for a wee job on the Volvo. The garage-man stayed thrawn and threatened to take him to court. So Ewan paid up, in the end.

'There was a dozen cars for sale parked in a row at the side of the garage. That night . . . it was decided later that a leak must have developed in one car, the furthest up the slope. Petrol ran down under the whole row and somehow ignited. The fire spread to the building. The whole shebang burned to the ground.'

'We passed it,' Tony said.

'There were suspicions by the dozen but not a damn bit of proof. And that's not the only such thing. Now do you see?' Carmichael demanded. 'When you came here before, I didn't hold back because he's like a brother to me. No, it was because I was feared to tell you where he was and feared not to warn him. And that's the whole truth of it. I'm sick sorry that I ever met the man and if you can take him away out of my life I'll be nothing but thankful.'

Carmichael leaned back tiredly in the corner of the settee. Evidently he felt that he had shot his bolt.

Mr Munro felt otherwise. 'Where will the mannie be away to now?' he asked sharply.

Carmichael sat up again and bristled with some of his earlier irascibility. 'How in hell would I ken a thing like yon?'

Mr Munro poked a bony finger at him. 'You ken the man and that's more than we do. Listen, now. Soon there'll be a ring round Grampian. With the sea to the east, more sea and the Moray Firth to the north and the hills to the south and west, there's not so many roads out.

'So if he's a damn bit of sense he'll go to ground, until the hunt's died down or until he's found a way out. So where's the most likely place for him to go and lie up? Where does he know? We have to find him soon or he'll switch vehicles and get clear.'

Carmichael closed his eyes. He was silent for so long that I thought that he had fallen asleep. I gave my cramped fingers another massage.

'When he went off on business,' Carmichael said, so suddenly that I jumped, 'he was gone for the working week. But sometimes he went away for a weekend.'

'To a hotel?' Tony asked. 'With a woman?'

'I don't think it. He brought his fancy-women here, to Mowdiemoss, and a fine clatter that made! But there was another mannie came looking for him one day, a round-faced man with silver hair. I call to mind that he was tall but with a stoop. I saw a key pass. My guess would be that Banks had the use of a place. I have the notion that he made his confidential phone calls from there. He said once, just a week or two back, that he thought his phone here might be tapped. Would that have been your lot?' he asked slyly.

'Certainly not,' Tony said indignantly. I wondered whether to believe him; whether, indeed, he would have known. The police are rarely given permission to tap a phone – it was a frequent complaint of Ian's – and then usually in connection with national security, but illegal phone-taps are not entirely unknown to them.

Mr Munro jerked us back to the point. 'Where is this place?' he snapped.

'I was never invited along,' Carmichael said. 'If it's any help, a bit later than this time last year he went off for the weekend. He said, "I'll maybe go to the Games."'

Ian's sandy eyebrows went up. 'He didn't say "the *somewhere* games"?'

Carmichael shook his head.

'There are Highland games all over the place at this time of year,' Tony said.

'Most of them,' said Mr Munro, 'are given the place name, just as you said. The Aboyne Games. The Ballater Games. And so on. But when folk say just "the Games", they mostly mean the Braemar Highland Games, because it's the biggest and the royal family are usually – yes?' he added as Carmichael made a muffled noise.

'I wouldna ken about yon,' Carmichael said. 'I've more to do with my time than watch a damned lot of caber tossing and fancy dances. But I mind now he said something more. He said, "I'll give Lizzie a wave." At the time,

I thought nothing of it, just that Lizzie was someone he knew.'

'You think that he meant Her Majesty?' Mr Munro sounded profoundly shocked.

'I can only tell you what he said,' Carmichael retorted. 'What he meant is up to you. But I mind when he came back that time he said he'd been at "the Gathering".'

'That's Braemar for sure,' Tony said. 'But it's still a long shot. Even if he was going to Braemar, that may not have been his regular haunt.'

'On the other hand,' said Ian, 'we have to be some-where and Upper Deeside is as likely as anywhere. It gives us a chance to be handy when something breaks.' I could see that he was itching to be on the move, in any direction if only he could believe that Foster was somewhere ahead.

Before agreeing, Tony subjected Carmichael to a further ten minutes of inquisition without obtaining any-thing further of use. 'You,' Tony told him at last, 'stay where we can reach you. In fact, if you leave the house you may as well drive yourself to Lodge Walk and save me the trouble of fetching you.' I looked a question at him. 'Aberdeen City Police used to be based on Lodge Walk,' he explained. 'Grampian Police are on a new site but the old name sticks.'

'I've no car,' the game dealer pointed out.

'Then walk. And pray that we get him before he does more damage. Otherwise we'll meet again in an interview room.'

It was several minutes before we got away, because first Tony, then Ian and finally Mr Munro insisted on reading Carmichael a lecture about questionable behaviour in the past perhaps being overlooked if he stayed out of mischief and passed us every fragment of information that he learned or remembered. I kept my mouth firmly shut. Then Ian insisted on a quick tour of the premises while Mr Munro, who had an elderly bladder, commandeered the use of Carmichael's toilet.

We met up at the car. Carmichael was watching from his front window. To judge from the bristling of his beard, he had recovered much of his truculence. Mac greeted us with what by comparison was almost adoration. 'I'm glad to see you too,' I told him.

Chapter Eight

'Let's move,' Tony said. 'If we hang around here we'll be called in and I'll get caught up in the creaking machinery of the investigation. I'll report in once we're too far up the road to be worth calling back. If they want answers they can have them – by radio.'

The back of Mr Munro's neck exuded disapproval of this cavalier treatment of the rules, though I seemed to remember that his own strict adherence to the book had on occasions only lasted for as long as the book happened to agree with his own intentions. We set off through mixed farmland, cutting across country on narrow and twisting roads. As Tony explained, once away from the coast the north–south roads are few and mostly minor. As we climbed onto the broad ridge that separates the valleys of the Don and the Dee, radio conditions picked up and Tony could think of no excuse for procrastinating any longer. He called Control and dictated a brief report. It received a curt acknowledgement but, to our surprise, provoked no other reaction.

We descended into the valley of Royal Deeside and set off westwards, parallel to the north bank of the river. We had emerged from forestry and were running through fertile farmland again.

By then, I think that we were all beginning to wonder if we had jumped to a rash conclusion. 'God, but I hope we've made a good guess,' Tony said fretfully. 'Mr Goth told me to help you, but I may have gone too far. If, on top of the rest, we're haring off in the wrong direction, I'll be lucky if I get away with a bollocking. Excuse me,' he added in my direction.

'Don't apologize,' I said. 'I agree with you.'

I had been looking out at the scenery, watching the hills approach closer and the scattered woodlands change from silver birch to predominantly conifers. 'Stop the car,' I said suddenly.

Mr Munro chose a place where he could pull safely onto a broad verge and halted the car. 'What is it?' he asked patiently.

'Those trees,' I said. 'What's that cotton wool looking stuff?'

The trees, I think, were geans – wild cherries. They looked distinctly moth-eaten and were dusted with white.

'Och, it's only a beastie does that. The caterpillar of the codling moth. There are other places you can see it, but lately it's shown itself mostly on Deeside, they say, and only on geans and elder. There was an article about it in the *Press and Journal* a whilie back.'

'Is this the time for a nature lesson?' Tony demanded irritably.

'Hold on.' I got out of the car and took a closer look. The cotton wool was slightly sticky. There were also white chrysalises.

I got back into the car. 'Drive on,' I said. 'And you, Tony, can start to breathe again. There were traces of that white stuff on Mr Foster's Volvo. That is assuming that this caterpillar really is special to Deeside?'

'Nowhere else nearer than Perthshire,' said Mr Munro, pulling out. Tony, as advised, breathed again. 'I think,' Mr Munro added.

Soon we were running through conifers with only occasional farmland. The encroaching hills loomed closer beyond the trees, massive enough to collapse under their own weight. They looked barren but I guessed that they would be splashed with the pinkish purple of the heather within a few weeks.

The radio came alive. Tony, still deep in forebodings, picked up the microphone and answered, but we could all hear the message. Officers at Crathie, who had been assisting the security officer in connection with the Queen's expected attendance at Sunday service, had seen a vehicle answering the description of Mr Carmichael's huge estate car, heading on up towards Braemar. They had been on foot and unable to follow. All vehicles were being stopped before reaching the snow gates at Braemar and other road blocks were being established.

Mr Munro began to burn up the road. Tony's smile of relief seemed to reach round to the back of his neck.

We could have saved time by cutting through the Pass of Ballater. Foster had already passed Ballater when he was seen at Crathie, but he might have doubled back along the South Deeside road, so we threaded through the small town. There was no overgrown dark red estate car, with or without a nudge bar, in the streets or in the car park behind the church.

We set off again on the last seventeen miles to Braemar. I think that we were all willing the car on, caught up in the 'rapture of pursuing' although Foster (as we were still calling him) had passed that way more than an hour earlier. There was a traffic car now below Crathie Church, too late. Balmoral Castle was no more than a glimpse of an ornate granite tower peeping over the trees.

It was as we ran through Braemar and saw ahead of us the end of a tailback from the roadblock that a sense of purposelessness overtook each of us in turn. Our quarry, with Dad's fortune beside him, was probably not more than a few miles off. He would be searching for, and perhaps finding, a way out of the trap; but we had done all that we could. Police routine was better equipped for a search than we were.

It had been a long morning. Lunch was long overdue. A meal would have been available at Mrs Jamieson's house, but we had passed within a few miles of it half an hour earlier and it would have been against our instincts to turn and drive away from the focus of the hunt. We found a small tearoom. The place was empty during the hiatus between lunch and tea and the staff were on their break, but the manageress was not inclined to turn away customers. While she prepared a scratch meal for us, Tony returned to the car and used his radio to report our position.

There was a payphone between the toilets. I used the last of my phonecard in calling home. Bruce, Mother told me, was thriving. Dad was responding well but fretful. Uncle Ronnie had been released from hospital; he could have driven a car and he was keen to know where we were so that he could join us. My uncle was a dangerous enough driver at any time, and I was appalled by a mental picture of him taking a long drive, one-footed, in a strange car and then starting to throw his weight around with the local police. I gave Mum a vague but reassuring message for Dad and then got her to call Uncle Ron to the phone. I told him very firmly that keeping an eye on the shoot was more important than the pursuit (an argument which he was predisposed to accept) and that until Mr Foster was caught he should sleep at Briesland House and spend as much time as possible doing guard duty.

We were marking time and hating it.

We finished our scanty meal and sat on over coffee, arguing testily as to whether there were no faint trails that we had missed. We had almost agreed to retrace our tracks and put the unfortunate Carmichael through the wringer again, when our tentative plans were tossed back into the melting pot. Tony's radio report had drawn the big wheels down on us.

Detective Chief Superintendent Goth was again without the retinue of subordinates customary for very senior officers engaged on major inquiries. This time he lacked even a humble sergeant. Instead, he had with him a man in his fifties, whom he introduced as Mr Bentligger, 'from St Andrews House'. Mr Bentligger was red-faced and rather roly-poly, with thinning silver hair. His suit, of quality cloth, was well cut and looked brand new; his tie, I thought, was from one of the Oxford colleges. He looked as though nature had intended him to be a jolly man but when success came in at the door the weight of responsibility had squeezed jollity out of the window. His expression was pensive and rather stern, matching that of Mr Goth.

Mr Bentligger listened intently while Mr Goth took Tony through a minute by minute inquisition about our morning's activities. Tony reported in scrupulous detail, omitting only the one uncomfortable fact that we had seen and ignored one very dead body. It was evident that Tony's messages had been fully relayed to the DCS and I was in no doubt that Mr Bentligger already knew the story of the robbery at Briesland House.

'I shall want your written report,' Mr Goth said at last.

'You shall have it, sir,' Tony said.

'And a transcript of your interview with the man Carmichael,' Mr Goth added. I realized suddenly that I would be expected to read my own shorthand and produce the transcript. With Ian's help and aided by his remarkable memory, I assured myself.

From a heavy briefcase, Mr Goth produced an envelope and from the envelope he took a Polaroid photograph and placed it on the table. It showed the handle of Dad's kris. The handle took up most of the photograph but I judged that it had been taken while the blade was still in place. My inadequate lunch seemed heavy, all of a sudden. 'Have any of you seen this before?' he asked sharply.

'Yes,' I said quickly, before Tony could put his foot in it. 'I have.' Tony was sitting opposite me and I saw his eyes pop open.

'You have?'

'Or one very similar. It was among the guns and other weapons stolen from my father's house.'

Tony had lost his colour but at least his eyes had returned to normal. He leaned back in his chair, breathing deeply.

'Could you identify it positively?' Mr Goth asked me.

'Not from a photograph. Let me have it in my hands and I'll tell you for sure.'

Mr Goth nodded.

The man from St Andrews House spoke for the first time. 'Don't pussyfoot around,' he said. 'Get on with it.'

I had been wondering why another civilian was accompanying a senior police officer on a murder inquiry, but it came to me that local police forces were responsible to the Scottish Secretary through one of the departments of the Scottish Office – the Scottish Home and Health Department, I rather thought. Mr Bettligger was probably the head cook and bottlewasher responsible for the Personal Income Investigation Branch, familiarly known as the Sleaze Squeeze.

Mr Goth hesitated for no more than the catch of a breath. Or perhaps he sighed. He was looking at Tony. 'Can you assure me that you have not seen this before?' he asked.

Tony's hesitation was even briefer. His colour was returning. He kept his face calm although, across the table, I could feel the tension in him. 'Yes, sir,' he said. And we were committed.

'Nor the body?' Mr Goth persisted.

Tony met his eye. I thought that a signal was passing between them. Tony shook his head.

'It has been suggested that you found the body and failed to report it.'

'Suggested by who?'

'That is not relevant.'

'I have a right to face up to anyone who makes such allegations against me,' Tony said, almost under his breath.

143

'All in good time.'

I looked quickly at Mr Goth but not in time to see whether he had glanced at the man from the Scottish Office. Instead, he had locked eyes with Tony McIver and I thought that a warning had passed, but in which direction I could not be sure.

'Well? I'm taking this very seriously. Answer the question.'

'I did not find the body,' Tony said firmly. I suppose that it was true. I was the one who had made the discovery.

'Can you say the same?' Mr Goth demanded of Ian.

Ian hesitated for a microsecond. Being caught out in a lie to a senior officer would have finished his career. But he had given his promise. 'I can,' he said.

Luckily, nobody thought to ask me. I was quite prepared to lie my head off, but I have never been able to lie with conviction.

Before he could be asked in his turn, Mr Munro got to his feet. 'I must pay a visit,' he said. 'I think that I saw a sign pointing to the Gents. We older gentlemen are not so strong in the bladder as you younger laddies.' His lanky form headed for the door.

'Can you explain how you came to find the place and not the body?' Mr Goth asked Tony.

'I understand that the body was in an outbuilding,' Tony said carefully. 'The house was empty and we had heard a vehicle driving off. We suspected that the man Carmichael had phoned a warning to his friend. It was a fair assumption that our man was making his escape by way of the farm-tracks. Mr Munro's car was not suitable for a cross-country pursuit. We decided to go back and question Mr Carmichael while his memory was still fresh, leaving the local lad to look around.'

'And I suggest,' Ian put in, 'that events proved this to be the right line of action. We obtained a description of the car that Foster would be driving, which enabled you to bottle him in . . . I hope,' he added, spoiling the effect.

Mr Goth pondered quietly for some seconds and then stood up. 'We're not finished with this subject,' he said. 'But now that Hamish Munro has put the thought into my head . . .'

He walked out of the room. Mr Bentligger's eyes followed him and he seemed to stir in his chair.

'I'll tell you what I find very significant,' Tony said. He fell silent. It was quiet in the dingy tearoom but I could hear women's voices in the street outside.

Mr Bentligger settled in his chair, but without relaxing.

'Go on,' Ian said at last. 'What do you find so significant?'

'This ring, or syndicate, or whatever you care to call it.'

'Call it a ring,' said Ian.

Tony nodded. 'This ring, then. Consider the problems they faced. Somebody had to introduce a customer who needed to explain away a specific amount of cash, give or take a margin. Then they had to match the customer with goods which could be resold for about the right figure, had no history of recent transactions and could credibly have been inherited from a relative.'

'Or picked up for pennies at a car boot sale,' said Ian.

'I suppose that's the other option. But consider. They must have been on the lookout for anyone in a position of responsibility and liable to give in to temptation. But those would bc exactly the signs that the Personal Income Investigation Branch would be watching for.' Tony looked at Mr Bentligger. 'What do you think?' he asked abruptly.

Bentligger raised his eyebrows and shrugged.

I was sensing all sorts of undercurrents. Tony and Ian waffled on without quite saying anything for a minute or two, until Mr Munro came back into the room wearing an expression of satisfaction which I considered excessive for the circumstances. He glanced at Tony, who got quickly to his feet. 'My turn,' he said and hurried out.

Mr Bentligger also began to get up. Mr Munro pressed him gently back into his chair with a hand on his shoulder. 'It is only a two-person shunkie,' he said. 'You'll need to tie a knot or go out the back.'

Such vulgarity was so out of keeping for the prim Highlander that I stared at him. He met my look blandly. A moment later Mr Goth came back and took his seat, followed after a few seconds by Tony. Mr Bentligger seemed to have lost the urge to go.

To my surprise, and I think the surprise of each of the others, Mr Goth did not pursue the subject of whether any of us had seen the body. 'I did not come here to discuss the shortcomings of one of my sergeants,' he said loftily. 'I have something else to say which is too confidential for the radio. There are too many transistor sets around these days which can receive the police wavebands and any crook on the run knows to listen in.

'The facts are these. You three can go home to Fernie-brae, or continue grubbing for clues to the whereabouts of the buried treasure if you like, provided that you stay away from the vicinity of Inverlaggan. In fact, stay out of

Glen Laggan altogether. But I shall need Sergeant McIver
tonight. I seem to remember that you have qualified to
carry a firearm?'

Tony agreed, expressionless.

'Good. You see, a rescue helicopter was up this way,
looking for a missing climber who turned up safe at
Glenshee. It was diverted to overlook this area and we
got a report of a man seen parking a vehicle of the right
description, tucked between two outbuildings at a sup-
posedly deserted farmhouse west of Inverlaggan Lodge.
For the moment, it's enough that we have a roadblock
where the Glen Laggan road comes out. It will take time
to gather up enough officers trained in firearms, beside
which the usual drill is to go in early in the morning,
when life's at its lowest ebb.'

'Is that really necessary?' Mr Munro asked.

'Certainly it is. You think I'm taking a sledgehammer
to crack a nut? On the contrary. He's known to be a
violent man. We don't know that he's alone. And, finally,
the last positive news that we have of him was that he
was in possession of more than a hundred firearms. How
many of those would be shootable, Mrs Fellowes?'

'Given the materials, almost all of them,' I said.

'And effective?'

'Many of them would be as effective as modern
weapons,' I told him. 'Just slower to reload.'

'With a hundred guns to choose from, who needs to
reload?'

I was about to point out that a non-shooting antique
dealer would be very unlikely to have a supply of black
powder, percussion caps and either shot or suitably sized
lead balls, but Mr Goth spoke on without a break. 'Armed

officers will go in at three a.m. With luck, Mrs Fellowes, as well as taking a killer into custody, they may recover your father's guns.'

'Well, good!' was all that I could find to say. It sounded very satisfactory and yet something inside me refused to relax just yet.

'I'm glad that the matter is nearing a satisfactory resolution,' Mr Bentligger said. 'I hope that all goes well. You'll keep me advised on anything you can get regarding others in the network?'

'Of course,' Mr Goth said.

'Then I think that I should be getting back to Edinburgh.'

'Of course,' Mr Goth repeated. 'If you'll come with me, I'll have the Sergeant drive you to the train.'

There was a general stirring and gathering of possessions. 'I'll see you in the morning,' Tony McIver said to me. 'I'll hope to be able to tell you that Mr Calder's property is safe.'

Mr Munro, Ian and I were left to our own devices. The lady who owned or ran the tea shop was hovering with the bill, anxious to clear our table for the teatime rush. We went outside and settled in Mr Munro's car.

'Did you ever get a feeling that your teeth didn't quite fit into your face?' Ian asked.

'I used to know the feeling well, when I had teeth,' Mr Munro said. 'It meant that something was not quite right. Now I am getting it again.' He drove round two corners and came back to the main road. The end to the tailback was in sight again. 'I thought as much,' he said. 'Either Murdo Goth has no faith in his own information or there is something fishy here. Shall we take a look at the bottom of Glen Laggan?'

'Better not,' Ian said.

'You're right. In that case there seems to be little we can do until this is over and done. I suggest that we go home and persuade Mary to give us something rather more substantial to eat. A good meal and a night's sleep seem to be called for. I have a feeling that we may be busy again tomorrow.'

Ian and Mr Munro kept up a constant if desultory chatter about policing in the Borders all the way back to Ferniebrae, effectively excluding me from participation. Comforting myself with the thought they could not avoid me for ever, I gave my attention to Mac.

Mr Munro was quick to point out that he had perforce neglected many of the chores about the smallholding. As soon as the promised meal had been eaten, he made himself scarce for the little that was left of the day and Ian, who usually avoids anything resembling gardening as he would a social disease, decided to lend him a hand. They seemed determined to deny me a chance of discussing the more puzzling aspects of the day's doings, but I managed to catch Mr Munro on his own as he enjoyed the late evening sun outside his front door.

'I want to ask you something,' I told him.

'Ask away,' he said comfortably. 'I'm not promising to answer.'

'What did you say to Mr Goth to make him let Tony off the hook?' I asked.

'I'll tell you that much,' he said, grinning his skull-like grin. 'As it happened, I did not have to say a thing to him. I was just about to remind him of a time when I was a sergeant and he was a lowly constable and I learned that he had called in sick because he had a date to take some lassie for a picnic. But before I could say a word, he told me that he knew dashed well that we were all guilty as hell – his words, not mine – but that he was not going to make an issue of it. He said that rules were made to be broken when the cause was good. And that,' he added indignantly, 'is one piece of philosophy that he did not learn from me.'

'I can remember a time when you threw the book away,' I told him. And I hurried on before he could seize on the chance to change the subject. 'What else was going on? There was more being understood than was being said aloud.'

The grin returned, toothier than ever. 'There still is,' he said. 'Sleep well.' He turned and went into the house.

I helped Mary Jamieson to wash up and set the table for breakfast. When I came back to our room from the bathroom, Ian was already in bed and pretending to be asleep. Or perhaps he really was asleep. It made no difference, because I knew of one sure way to wake him up without annoying him more than very slightly.

I lay against the curve of his back. When I was sure that I had his attention I asked him what he thought had been said in the toilet of the tearoom.

'What are you suggesting?' Ian was pretending to be shocked.

'Nothing scurrilous,' I told him, 'and damn well you know it. But don't tell me that the sudden rush to the Gents was for real. Or is there an outbreak of cystitis among the police and are you going to come down with it? From the moment that Mr Goth arrived in the tea-room, nobody seemed to mean what they were saying or say what they meant. And you were as bad as the others. What was it all about?'

'You saw and heard as much as I did. All right,' he said quickly when I began to squeeze where I had been stroking. 'My guess would be that they're still hoping that the search and roadblocks will find him but, wherever he is, the farmhouse near Inverlaggan Lodge is not the place.'

'That's what I thought. So it's a trap?'

'That's my guess. Don't stop doing that,' he added. 'I could get to like it.'

For the moment, his little pleasures were secondary so far as I was concerned, but I continued while I thought about the idea of a trap. A trap can only work if the mouse finds his way to the cheese. 'That rubbish that you and Tony were talking, it was just calculated to keep Mr Bentligger in his chair. So it's a trap for Mr Bentligger?' I suggested.

'They want the man at the Scottish end who's been introducing bribe-takers to the ring. They want him almost as much as they do Foster. In fact, they want them both. When you have two suspects in custody, you can nearly always get one of them to talk—'

'By kidding each of them that the other is already spilling the beans?'

'Such has been known.' Ian tried to turn and face me but I kept my grip on him. After a few seconds he went on, 'I think Mr Goth was using the chance to pass infor-mation to Bentligger, not to us. It's the only way that it makes sense. And, of course, if Bentligger is a big noise

151

with the Personal Income Investigation Branch, he would be very well placed to sniff out whoever was taking the biggest backhanders. And he would then very much not want Foster to be taken into custody and interrogated.'

'But surely,' I said, 'if Bentligger is the Scottish Mr Big who's been seeking out the clients for the sleaze-laundering, he'd know where Foster's second home is, or at least the phone number.'

I felt Ian shrug. 'In that case, nothing would have been lost. But Foster seems to be a compulsively secretive man. He's been very careful to cover his tracks and if he has a pied-à-terre somewhere it's because he wanted a complete break between here and there. So why would he leave himself open to betrayal if one of his cronies gave himself away? And Mr Goth didn't get to be Detective Chief Superintendent by missing tricks.' Ian made another effort to turn over and this time I let him. 'I'd bet my month's pay against your month's housekeeping that Foster's mobile doesn't work any more.'

'And that any phone calls Mr Bentligger makes, or tries to make, will be tapped?'

'I doubt whether they'd risk asking for authorization. He's well known in Edinburgh. It could get back to him.'

'But they'll be tapped anyway?'

'That would be naughty.'

At a rough count I had a hundred and fourteen more questions to ask, but my method of wakening Ian had had a rather more extreme effect than I had intended. We were both beginning to lose interest in Messrs Foster and Bentligger, the Sleaze Squeeze and even Dad's guns . . .

Chapter Nine

I awoke from a deep and contented sleep to another morning of bright sunshine. It was early, I knew, because the sunlight was shining almost horizontally across the dormer window, but Ian was already out of bed and struggling into his clothes.

'You'd better get up,' he said. 'Something's afoot. I can hear Tony McIver's voice and he's in a bit of a tizzy.'

With that, he was out of the room and rumbling down the stairs. I was as anxious as anybody over the possibility of bad news or to receive glad tidings – and probably more so. Ian and I were contented enough. We lacked nothing that a reasonable person might want. If my inheritance was lost for ever, we would still be immensely rich by the standards of three-quarters of the world's population. But the wealth represented by the missing guns represented in turn my parents' security in old age. It could also in time buy for me the one worthwhile thing that money can buy – freedom from having to worry about money.

Nobody was going to see me with my hair in a tangle and no makeup. However, putting aside any temptation to turn over and go back to sleep, I managed to wash, dress and make myself moderately presentable within seven or eight minutes which, for me, was the equivalent of the three-minute mile.

When I made my more decorous descent of the stairs I found that, although a delicious smell of frying bacon was coming from the kitchen, when I looked into the room I saw that the bottled gas had been turned off under the pan. The house seemed to be deserted. I emerged from the front door to discover why. For a start, Mr Munro's Rover, the apple of his eye, was no longer in its usual place on its own rectangle of granite chips opposite the door. Then I saw that Mr Munro, his sister, my husband and Tony McIver were grouped in the road beyond the small police car in which Tony must have arrived. They were examining an enormous dark red estate car and they looked as bemused as I felt. I walked round the front of the strange vehicle. There was slight damage to the front of it and traces of paint on the nudge bar which could have come from our car. There were also no less than three small bullet-holes, but I refrained from pointing them out, merely reserving the fact of their presence for Dad, next time that he should criticize my marksmanship. Nobody was speaking.

Mary Jamieson broke the silence. 'You'll do no good standing here gowping,' she said. 'Breakfast in five minutes.' She went into the house.

'I was arriving here, mostly to tell you about last night,' Tony said, 'and there it was, looking so much in place that I nearly walked past. I've reported it and a team from Forensics will be out to deal with it – and a fat lot of good may it do them. They'll end up proving that Foster was the last person to drive it, and we know that anyway. I've reported your car missing,' he told Mr Munro. 'But he won't go far with it.'

'I should hope not,' Mr Munro said. 'I suppose it's too much to hope that he won't bad-use it?'

'There's always hope.'

Mr Munro looked as though he had found half a worm in what remained of his apple. His car could be replaced or repaired, but it would not be the same. 'Or set fire to it?' he suggested.

'That might depend on whether or not he wants to distract attention. He'll swap your car for another just short of a roadblock and go through before word gets there. That's what I'd do.'

'But what about the guns?' I asked.

'If he's managed to steal something like a long-chassis Land Rover,' Ian said, 'he may manage to take most of them along. Otherwise they'll be hidden. Or dumped. I doubt if they were stolen for profit – they'd be very difficult to dispose of without leaving a trail that would bring the wrath of several governments and umpteen police forces about his ears.'

'You mean, he's put us through all this just for spite? Dad and Uncle Ronnie in hospital?'

'That's my reading of it,' Ian said. 'It's funny,' he added musingly, 'that Mr Goth mentioned buried treasure.'

I felt my spirits sink. Dad's fortune might be buried on some moor, to rust away where we could never find it.

Tony ducked into the police car and came out with a map of the area. He spread it on the roof of the car and we gathered round. 'Foster managed to drive here without being stopped. He'd have been taking an awful risk if he used the A roads, rather less on the B roads, but we certainly couldn't watch every dirt-track in the area. There are more than enough estate roads, foresters' tracks, farm roads, routes to grouse drives or down to the fishing, and some of them link up or come close enough that a man with a good map and a four-wheel-drive could get from one to the other.'

Ian leaned closer. 'So, backtracking from here, where could he have started from?'

'Offhand, I can see about six possible routes—' Tony was interrupted by the radio installed in the car. He ducked inside again. 'Your car's parked outside the Invercauld Hotel,' he told Mr Munro when he straightened up. 'I'm told that it seems to be undamaged. And there's a motorcyclist, who had been camping beside the Dee, complaining that his bike vanished during the night along with his helmet and a complete set of leathers. Our friend's away over the mountains by now.'

'But we are still looking—' I began.

'For your father's guns. I know that,' Tony said patiently. 'But at least he can't have taken them all with him on a motorbike – if I'm right in guessing that Foster's the bike-snatcher. We now have time to eat a civilized breakfast and then tackle the question methodically.'

'I can go along with that,' Ian said, turning towards the house. I followed. Mr Munro, who would have preferred to rush to recover his cherished car but had perforce to wait for a lift, sighed and came along.

'But you came to bring us up to date?' Ian said. 'We were fairly sure that all the flapdoodle was a trap set to see whether Mr Bentligger was in on the corruption deals.'

Tony McIver paused outside the door. 'You were right, except that he had been suspect for some months and suspicion became certainty when he turned up and began interfering almost as soon as Foster came unstuck. What was wanted was proof. So I was given my orders in Bentligger's presence. When we spoke in the cludgie, all Mr Goth said was that I should play along and ignore all side-issues.'

Mary Jamieson served a generous breakfast in her kitchen. 'There was a message,' she told Ian. 'You're to phone your office.' She went out into the garden and left us in privacy.

Mr Munro brought his mind back from anxiety about his beloved Rover. 'Did you get the proof?' he asked.

Tony nodded violently and emptied his mouth. 'Bentligger headed straight for a public phone and tried to call Foster's mobile. Then he called another number. We lay in wait at the deserted farmhouse. Soon after dark, three men arrived in a borrowed Land Rover; they'd come over the moor to bypass the roadblock they thought was at the road end. They'd come to get Foster out, of course, but what they got instead was nabbed. Two were from Dundee and one from Perth and they must be the heavies Foster called on when there was dirty work to be done. The younger of the Dundee pair's a poor craitur and he'd already started to spill his guts when I came away. He says that Bentligger told them where you were staying.

'They had the number of the phone at Foster's secret den, which Bentligger didn't, so when they reached the farmhouse and found that he wasn't there, they called it on a mobile of their own. Just before we moved in, that was. He told them, too late, that they'd walked into a trap and to get the hell out of it, but he was very interested to hear from them where you were staying.'

'A piece of dashed impertinence, coming here to pinch my car,' Mr Munro snorted.

'Spite again, more likely,' Tony said. 'And perhaps a hint that he wasn't finished quite yet.'

Hope was bubbling up inside me. 'But if we know the phone number,' I said, 'surely you can get the address.'

Tony looked at me sadly. 'I hate to break it to you. But they only had the number on a scrap of paper which they took along with them. Foster told them to burn it, so that's what they did.'

'And none of them can remember it?'

'They're not the type to memorize things,' Tony said. 'We're trying to get the number from the records of the phone call, but it seems that their mobile was a stolen one, rechipped, and God alone knows where the cost of the call will fetch up.'

I nearly said that maybe we weren't *meant* to recover those damn guns but I swallowed the words. Everything had started to roll our way; surely we could still get over the occasional stumbling block. Perhaps the technicians in Forensic Science would find mud on one of the cars peculiar to some tiny glen . . .

It was a breakfast which deserved to be lingered over, but we were hot for the chase again. Foster might have escaped the net, but Dad's guns – my inheritance – were still around. We ate quickly, cleared the dishes into the sink and spread Tony's maps on the table.

It was soon clear that although Foster could have come from the Braemar area making use of several bits of minor road, he would have had to risk the main North Deeside road for some miles or detour over some particularly mountainous moors. 'We need a larger scale map,'

Tony said, 'and some local knowledge.' He put his finger on the map. 'For instance, this is almost a route but we don't know if he could drive that monster from *here* to *here*. If so, he could have started from somewhere round Marbuie. Or look here . . .'

'I'd better make that phone call,' Ian said. 'Then we can tackle it methodically and wherever we're in doubt we can go and look.'

'The local sergeant's a member of the Mountain Rescue,' said Tony. 'He can probably save us a lot of off-road motoring. I'll give him a call.'

Ian was at the phone for several minutes, long enough for me to satisfy myself that the process of elimination was not going to be easy. But when he came back, Ian was grinning all over his face. My ever mercurial spirits, which had been falling again, rose once more.

'The Professor came up trumps,' Ian told me. 'That tick that you took off Mac. The Prof astonished even himself. He says that he's going to do a paper about it for the Forensic Science Society.'

'He found some significant DNA?' I suggested, to jog him along a bit.

'DNA testing takes time,' Ian said. 'But he did find some unusual cells. He'll confirm his results from genetic fingerprints later, but already he's ninety-nine per cent sure that before the tick attached itself to Mac its last host had been an angora goat.'

We were in full cry again. No matter that Mac, with or without his master, might have paid only a fleeting social call on the goats (and some time earlier at that, as I

159

remembered the life and habits of the sheep-tick); we felt, almost knew, that we were right this time.

The Braemar police station, I now discovered, was not manned full-time. Tony's first attempt at a phone call ended up in Stonehaven, miles away on the North Sea coast. A call to the Braemar post office was more informative. But several smallholders in the area, it seemed, kept goats and our informant could not have told an angora from the Tirolean Mountain variety. She was a lady of initiative, however, and helpful with it, and could be heard asking the question of the customers in the shop. It took her only a few seconds to establish that the only angora goats known in the Braemar area were kept by a certain Willy Paterson at Bonnypark. Tony wrote down directions. As he listened to the lady, I saw the light of a great understanding spread across his face.

I was in no hurry to get my hopes too high. 'You're sure that we're right this time?' I asked as he disconnected. 'Or is this another wild-goose chase?'

'Judge for yourself,' Tony said. 'The man's an artist. A painter.' He saw that the information had no significance for me, although the others seemed to be following him, and went on, 'Think about it. Foster had been buying second-rank paintings – very valuable but not widely known. His customers want to "discover" them. And where are valuable paintings most often discovered?'

The question was probably intended to be rhetorical but Ian, his voice exultant, answered for him. 'Under later paintings which have been made over the original. So when he bought his seascape by Whoosit—'

'E. W. Cook,' I said.

'—he needed a tame painter who could lay on a coat

of something not too difficult to dissolve and then do a daub on top. That's why he kept a secret hideout in the hills. Let's go.'

We fitted ourselves into the small police car. That act alone made me feel guilty; perhaps a residual emotion from all the prisoners who had gone before. Even Mac, sprawled across my lap again, seemed a little cowed. He had glanced at the big estate car and looked away quickly.

Once we were on the road, I said, 'It seems to me that the buyer wouldn't have much left of his bribe after paying off the painter as well as the members of the ring.'

'That doesn't follow,' Ian said over his shoulder. 'Off the top of the head, let's say that a man diverts a fat contract, to gain a backhander of – what? – say a hundred thousand. Auntie's willow-pattern commode turns out to be worth thirty grand, of which he loses ten to Foster and Company. He can buy the Ferrari that he always wanted, pay off his mortgage and bank the rest on the Continent. Who's going to add up the improvements in his lifestyle and work out that his windfall plus his savings couldn't have covered it?'

Little more than half an hour's driving brought us again to Braemar. Mr Munro's car was parked, as stated, outside the Invercauld Hotel. Also as stated, it looked undamaged; but there the accuracy of the report ended. When Mr Munro tried the key, nothing whatever happened. He raised the bonnet. Every single wire, even the connection to the windscreen washer, had been removed as also had the distributor cap and rotor arm.

'Why would a man do a thing like that?' Mr Munro demanded plaintively.

'He's a man with a massive capacity for hatred,' Ian said.

We waited, keeping impatience in check, while Mr Munro entered the hotel to phone his local garage. He returned with the cheering news that our car, although still in need of two new panels and a respray, was now driveable.

We returned as we had come, to where we had seen a signpost to Glendubh. Here, a narrow road which could have been mistaken for a firebreak set off through a thick fir wood for a hundred yards before emerging into a fringe of farmland. The road, single-track with passing places, followed the course of a wandering stream until both entered the mouth of a small valley. Where the sides were still shallow, the grassland continued on either side of the road before giving way to the ubiquitous rocks and heather above.

Ahead, the fields grew smaller. White dots grew into about thirty goats in a field although whether they were Angora I had not the least idea. But another sign, roughly painted, indicated that Bonnypark was the house and outbuildings that we could see beyond the goats, so Tony turned off and we bumped our way up a track that was not only uncomfortably steep but very rough, the rains of many winters having washed away much of the surface down to the underlying boulders. The ground behind the house seemed to be flat for a stone's throw and then rose abruptly in a craggy hillside where only heather and a few stunted trees managed to cling.

On my lap, Mac sat up and his tail began to thump on Ian's knee beside me. 'He's certainly been here before,' I said, 'for what that's worth. And enjoyed himself.'

'He probably lusts after the goats,' said Ian.

Tony parked as close to the small house as he could and we dismounted, but I left Mac in the car. He might have recognized the goats as just good friends; on the other hand he might be seeing them as a worthy quarry, to be chased and eaten.

Nobody came to the door to find out who had arrived, which was unusual in such surroundings if the house was occupied. Tony knocked on the door and we waited. There was still no answer and no sound from within. There could be a dozen normal explanations, but after happening on one dead body only the previous day I was predisposed to expect the worst. I began to feel an uneasiness in the vicinity of my upper bowel.

Tony tried the door. It opened under pressure and we saw that the lock had been forced. Paradoxically I found this reassuring, suggesting burglary rather than violence.

Ian echoed my thoughts. 'Foster would want to recover any canvas or canvases that had already been delivered for overpainting. That's one kind of valuable that he could carry on a motorbike.'

I could hear the sound of an engine. To give myself further reassurance, I looked around in the hope of seeing the figure of Willy Paterson working in the fields. There was another cottage on the other side of the valley and a large woman on a small tractor had descended through the field opposite the goats. She crossed the road and began the climb towards Bonnypark. While we waited, I used my eyes. Telephone wires and a heavier electrical cable, strung between poles, arrived at the house but I noticed that poles and wires went on around a shoulder of the hill. An even rougher version of the track followed a drystone wall in the same direction.

She jolted to a stop beside us at last and climbed off the tractor, red faced and beaded with sweat. She might have been a beauty some thirty years ago but time and the weather had not treated her kindly. Her clothing seemed to have been left over from when she had cast a smaller shadow. 'Whit's the polis daein' here?' she wanted to know. 'Is Wully a' richt? Dinna tell me there's ocht come o'er him.'

'Not so far as I know,' Tony said. 'He's away, is he?'

'Awa' tae his tittie in Balloch.' (In Scots, *tittie* can mean *sister.*) 'He'll be painting the loch. That aye pleases the tourists. I'm minding the gaits, till he's back.' She nodded towards the goats. 'Hey! Who's brak the door?'

'It would have been another man,' I said. 'A man who comes here sometimes, bringing that dog that's in our car. Where does that phone line go to?'

'Tae the caravan, in coorse.' She sniffed disapprovingly and looked in at Mac, to make sure that we were talking about the same dog. 'Yon mannie! That fair-faced, he is, but sleekit. Fills his car from my diesel tank if I turn my back! I telled Wullie I'd no trust the man as far as I could pish. And I'm a woman,' she added, in case we were in any doubt.

Tony, young and unmarried as he was, turned pink and Mr Munro was looking shocked. Ian, who was acclimatized to my occasional bouts of vulgarity, took over. 'When was he here last?' he asked.

'Somebody was there yestreen, efter sundoon. I seed him ootby, daein' something by the lichts o' a car. I thocht it'd be Wullie back.'

'Doing what?' I asked.

'Dinna ken. I'm no long-nebbit.' This last disclaimer of curiosity was immediately contradicted by her obvious intention of remaining to see what was afoot.

The caravan would be our first objective. We set off on foot along the continuation of the track but when the caravan came in view – a large but shabby static, set among rowans and silver birch – I turned back, on the excuse that I wanted to fetch Mac. My real reason was to tour the house and outbuildings without interference from the protective lady. This I did at speed, but it was sufficient to assure myself that no collection of guns was stored in any of the few rooms. What had once been a parlour had been converted for use as a studio and I saw at least one old stretcher from which the canvas had been removed. Such paintings as were on show were competent daubs. The remainder of the ground floor was a sitting room with a minute kitchen adjoining, and there was one bedroom under the eaves. The outbuildings were cluttered only with the paraphernalia of goat husbandry and attending to the garden at the side of the house where neat rows of vegetables were growing.

I pulled the door to behind me and fetched Mac from the car. He sat down and looked at the house door, his tail twitching. The artist, it seemed, had been a soft touch for handouts of food. I put his leash on him and we hurried after the others. This part of the track had not seen much recent use and grass was beginning to sprout in the ruts.

We found the others at the caravan. The door stood open as though inviting us to notice its emptiness, but the woman was protesting. 'The place is Wullie's,' she said. 'Yon rinagate only paid him a wee mailing. You've no right in there.'

'We've no need, either,' I said.

Tony nodded. 'There's been no vehicle along here for a week or more,' he said. 'Where did you see the lights?'

'By Wullie's hoose,' the woman said reluctantly.

'Leaving the caravan door open may have been meant to distract us from somewhere else,' Ian said.

Just to be sure, we walked around the caravan. The curtains were drawn back and we could see into every corner. The furnishings were simple, the place almost bare. Its appearance agreed with our supposition that Foster had used it for his more confidential business. It was possible although unlikely that the sparse furniture was concealing a gun or two, but no more than that. A thorough search by properly authorized detectives would undoubtedly follow. I knelt down to peer underneath, but there was nothing to be seen but a minimum of plumbing and some dead weeds and dried leaves blown by the wind. A small scorched area and some paper ash outside the door suggested that Foster had burned any records before leaving.

We returned to the cottage. 'Obviously the other man didn't have a key to the house?' Ian suggested.

The woman shook her head firmly. 'Wullie said not.'

'If he had a key, he wouldn't have had to break in,' I pointed out. A second later, I saw what Ian was getting at. 'Unless it was another piece of misdirection.'

'I'm going to take a look inside anyway,' Tony said.

'You bide out here,' the woman said indignantly.

'I'm sorry,' Tony said.

'I'll call the polis.' She had no sooner spoken than she

realized that she was standing beside a police car in livery. She pursed her lips and conjured up a more mighty threat. 'I'll tell Wullie when he gets hame!' I decided that the absent Willie was lucky in his friends.

'You should certainly do that,' Tony said. 'But if you have his sister's address, we'll have told him long before that.'

Her bolt shot, the woman gave in but glowered like a gargoyle. 'Just you, then,' she said. 'And mysel'. Naebody else.'

That seemed to be a fair compromise. Tony went inside while Ian and Mr Munro and I stayed in the sunshine. Mr Munro, a dedicated gardener, drifted towards the vegetables.

There was a tooting from below and the woman came out. 'Hey' she said. 'Yon's the baker's van. I maun chase. You're no to touch naethin', mind! I'll be back.' And she straddled the little tractor again and bounced off down the hill with many a backward glance to be sure that none of us was joining Tony indoors.

Tony came out after a few minutes, rather dustier than when he went in. 'Nothing,' he said.

'You tried the roof-space?' I asked.

'Nobody had been up there for years.'

'And under the floor?'

'There was a hatch under the doormat. Nothing there. Would anybody fancy a cup of tea while we have a little think? There's fairly fresh goat's milk to go with it.'

'Go ahead,' I told him. 'Goat's milk is good.'

Tony went back inside.

'Well, now,' Mr Munro said slowly. 'The mannie Foster left Mowdiemoss yesterday, one jump ahead of us. It's to be assumed that he had Mr Calder's guns with him in that red Yankee monstrosity of Carmichael's. The evidence suggests that he came here. This morning he dumped the big car on my doorstep, took my car into Braemar and stole a motorbike from there. He surely couldn't have hidden the guns at Ferniebrae without my knowing it?'

'It seems difficult to believe,' I said.

'Then can either of you suggest—'

'They've got to be here,' I said. 'Got to.'

Mr Munro shook his head sadly and verbalized my worst fears. 'If the mannie had spite enough to spoil my car, just for devilment, he may have dumped Mr Calder's guns along the way, in some quarry or a bog...'

'Hush a moment,' Ian said. 'What's that noise?'

We listened. There was a faint humming. 'Tony filling the kettle,' I suggested.

'Aye,' said Mr Munro. 'But yon's not pipe-noise. It's a pump. Drawing water up from the burn, likely.'

'*Not* likely,' Ian said. 'You can't suck water up more than about thirty-two feet. Any higher than that and you're just making a vacuum. We're a good bit higher than that above the stream. You can push water as high as the power of the pump lets you, but to do that the pump would have to be down at the bottom and we wouldn't be able to hear it. There has to be a well.'

The noise had stopped. I went to the kitchen window and told Tony to run the tap again. Ian and Mr Munro paced around with heads cocked to the side of their better ears. Near the corner of the house was a gap in the vegetables caused, I had thought, by the absent Wullie pulling greens for consumption. But when Mr Munro stepped off the path and onto that patch his footfall made a hollow sound.

'Aha!' Ian said. He hurried to the nearest outbuilding and came back with a spade. I went to the same place in search of string and wire. By the time that I returned with a ball of binder twine and a piece of fence-wire, Ian had uncovered some heavy boards and begun lifting them. The humming sound became louder. It seemed to me that somebody had shovelled a few inches of earth over a well-head which had been almost flush with ground level. The disturbed earth had soon dried to the colour of its surroundings in the fine weather. Wullie, on his return, might have noticed that the boards over his well-head were no longer showing; but it is surprising how invisible the familiar object can become.

Ian pried up the boards. The well had been solidly built many years before but it was only about a metre square. The water seemed to be about twenty feet below but I reminded myself that I was judging by the reflection of my own head in the top opening and that the water would be only half as far below me.

Ian's head was framed beside mine in the mirror below us. 'The water must be deep,' he said. 'If they're there. There's nothing showing.'

I made my piece of wire into a hook and dangled it on the twine, kneeling over the well without regard for my clothes. This was more important. I had to know. Sure enough it broke up the reflections in the water's surface at about ten feet down. Another four feet and I could feel my hook making contact. I jiggled until I felt it take a hold, lose it and catch again; and then I tried a steady pull.

My simple hook had caught the bolt of a Chassepot rifle. It came to my waiting hands and I dried it lovingly with my handkerchief. It might be one of the least valuable of the stolen guns, but it was strong evidence that the remainder were there to be saved. It had suffered a chip out of the butt but seemed otherwise undamaged. The water, I decided, must have cushioned its fall.

'He didn't intend to come back for them,' I said.

I got to my feet. I pecked Mr Munro on the cheek and kissed Ian as a wife should do. I was very close to tears. So when Tony came out of the house, carrying a tray of tea and goat's milk and wondering what the fuss was about, I was still thinking of Ian and I gave Tony a kiss that was far from sisterly and went on rather longer than Ian approved of, or so he said later. He was joking, I think.

Tony, who had missed almost all of his night's sleep, only yawned.

My first concern was the question of damage to the guns. Would they suffer more, I wondered, from continued immersion in fresh, soft water or from hasty and amateurish attempts at recovery? The question was resolved for me when Tony pointed out that the recovery of stolen goods was a matter for the police and that they had access to more sophisticated techniques for the purpose than I had. This I accepted on Tony's personal assurance that the well would be guarded and that the weaponry would be carefully handled, listed, preserved and forwarded to Newton Lauder as soon as the Procurator Fiscal could be persuaded to release them.

Suddenly we were in danger of being at a loose end. We had a celebratory drink in Braemar while Tony, finding the local cop-shop manned, dashed inside to set the wheels in motion. I phoned Mum with a message which should have ensured a good night's sleep for Dad. Bruce, she said, was hardly missing me at all.

A uniformed constable turned up with a police Range Rover. Tony was caught up in organizing the recovery of the guns, the obligatory reporting to Mr Goth and all the nuts and bolts of the murder and robbery cases and he sent his apologies. We were chauffeured back, to drop Mr Munro at Ferniebrae and onward to collect our car, battered but now safely driveable.

We called at the nearest shops, before making a final visit to Ferniebrae, to thank Mrs Jamieson for her hospitality and her brother for his help. We left what I felt was an inadequate gift, mostly of whisky which we knew that they both enjoyed, but I assured Mr Munro that whether or not the insurers coughed up the promised reward we would cover his loss of no-claims bonus. Mary Jamieson refused to let us go without eating one more meal and her brother insisted several times that if we could ever make use of his services again we were not to hesitate. As we left at last, the car weighed down with carrier bags of fruit and vegetables from the Ferniebrae garden, there was a sadness in my soul. Mr Munro, in all his guises between inspector and chief superintendent, had been a part of my childhood, my teens and my adult life. Sometimes he had been the bogeyman, sometimes a remote figure among Dad's companions, occasionally an honorary uncle. But I felt that I had never known him until now.

Our route took us near to Bonnypark so we threaded the single-track road one more time. I was easier in my mind when I saw that there were already several vehicles at the house and a bustle of men; and even from the distance we could see a stout female figure in attitudes of protestation, no doubt defending the property against the ravages of the police. If a single carrot from Wullie's garden was removed to augment supper in a police house or bunches of goat-hair abstracted for fly-tying, it would not be the fault of his protective lady-friend. We turned in the mouth of the track and set off back to the main road.

The Cairn o' Mount road had unhappy associations. We went back by Glenshee over what had once been the Devil's Elbow. Ian resigned himself to having the use only of the door mirror while I angled the interior mirror to give me a view to the rear; but there was no sign that we were being followed again.

We turned off the main road to Newcastle and again off the B-road to Newton Lauder and fetched up at Briesland House in early evening.

Chapter Ten

There could be no doubt that I would be entering one of the busiest periods of my life, so it was agreed that Ian and I would stay at Briesland House indefinitely, occupying my old room and displacing Uncle Ronnie who was hobbling around with one ankle in strapping. Briesland House was spacious in the Victorian manner, but the devoting of two large rooms to a workbench and the stock and collection of antique guns had seriously depleted the bedroom space. My uncle was banished to what had once been a maid's bedroom above the kitchen.

My mother had enjoyed having undisputed sway over her grandson but she had found the experience wearing. Also, Janet and Wal were impatient for her to take her turn again in the shop. I would have to resume caring for a baby who seemed to have forgotten who I was, while taking delivery of the guns as they were released by the police. However carefully Ian and his friends had cleaned them, a first priority would be to dismantle them where possible, bearing in mind that some screws and pins might have been in place for a couple of centuries or more, for a slow but thorough drying prior to beginning other repairs. With a little luck, a short period under fresh water would not have caused too much harm to well-oiled metal; but what would have happened to oil-finished walnut, or what damage had been done, despite the cushioning effect of the water, by dropping the guns on top of each other, I was afraid to imagine.

Then there was the imminent delivery of the pheasant poults to the family shoot. Dad, from his hospital bed, was still insisting that the new pen be brought into service. In one way he was right. The poults would regard the cover where they had lived from six weeks old as home; most would still be there when shooting began three or four months later and so the benefit of the new ground would be reaped. On the other hand, young pheasants needed a vast amount of tender care. They had to have food and water. They needed shelter. They should have roosts to go up to at night so that they could learn to roost out of reach of ground predators. If not kept busy and provided with secluded corners, feather-picking would almost certainly break out. And above all, they had to be kept safe from predators until they were old enough and wise enough to look after themselves – and not just foxes, which could be excluded from the release pens. Few cat-owners realized the damage that dear pussy could do when away from home. And even more problematic were buzzards and sparrowhawks, which were protected by law despite being present in almost plague numbers.

But we all buckled to, as far as we were able, and somehow we more or less coped, give or take the occasional panic.

The papers had heard about our loss, but the recovery of the guns, occurring just as the story leaked to them, robbed it of most of its news value. They printed the bare bones and the reporters bothered us very little. By the time the connection was made between the murder and the robbery, Mr Foster was yesterday's news.

Between us, Ian and I cooked up an acceptable transcript of the Carmichael interview.

Uncle Ronnie had called on a neighbouring head keeper and his assistant for help in return for past favours and the new pen had been finished even to the electric anti-fox wire around the base. But there were signs, he said, of sparrowhawks in the area.

Dad, who was making good progress but not yet ready to come home, had to be visited and reassured.

The first batch of guns, recovered, dried, oiled and photographed for evidence, arrived from Aberdeen by Securicor. I began work straight away on the first and most urgent task, which was to take them apart. Thanks to Dad's use of an age-old trick and filling with tallow any barrels that showed signs of serious pitting, there was little obvious rust damage, but hidden lockwork would be in serious danger. Most of the guns dismantled with relative ease but one German wheel lock with internal mechanism proved so recalcitrant that I had to drill the screws out. New and matching screws would have to be made, hardened and coloured later. A wipe with linseed oil would restore the surface of the woodwork once it had dried out.

I spent a whole day with an agent from the insurers. There was no argument over the cost of repairs. I managed to skate very lightly over the thin ice of the total value of the haul, easing my conscience with the thought that Dad's penny-pinching on the insurance would be reflected in the value of the reward. But when I dragged the discussion round to that subject, the agent pointed out that the reward was conditional on the arrest and conviction of the thieves. I argued that most of the thieves were already in custody although charged with a variety of other offences. Mr Foster was still at liberty.

'Very well,' the agent said, when he had the whole story. 'I quite see that the police are unlikely to go to the trouble and expense of trying to prove robbery while they're trying your Mr Foster for murder. If the men in custody are convicted of assault and Mr Foster is convicted of murder, and if at the same time the police assure us that they believe that those who were responsible for the theft of the guns are all being dealt with though not necessarily for that offence, the reward will be paid.'

At first I was despondent about the damage to the guns. Most of them had suffered damage by being dropped on to one another in the well. One of the most valuable items, a pair of flintlock duelling pistols by Wogden, had been deposited in the original case. This had saved the pistols and their accessories, but the leather case, on which much of the value depended, had suffered. I sent it to an Edinburgh leather-worker for an opinion. But my mind was relieved by a phone call from a collector, a regular client. He had the story of our loss and recovery and he asked about the condition of the guns in stock and in particular a double-barrel percussion Manton that he had admired on his last visit. I told him that the trigger guard was bent and there was a small dent in one barrel, so he would have to wait several weeks until Dad or I had time to carry out remedial work. I was about to offer a small discount when he broke in on me. 'Don't do that,' he said. 'The damage is part of its history. Before,

it was a gun of minor technical interest. Now it's a gun
with a story.'

I had finished dismantling and drying the first batch
of guns and was starting repairs to one of the client's
Holland and Hollands while awaiting delivery of the
remainder, when another phone message announced
that the pheasant poults would be delivered two days
later.

The previous year's release pens were ready and the
new pen needed little more than a supply of feed and
water.

Uncle Ronnie's ankle had swollen up again and it
happened that every other member of the family had
some inescapable commitment; so next morning I set off
without human companionship. Mac, who had attached
himself adoringly to me ever since he had discovered
that people can be kind to animals, insisted on coming
along. I also took along Ian's twelve-bore shotgun
although, as he pointed out, Mr Foster would certainly
have been out of the country long since and would have
to be insane to show his face again.

I was driving an old open-backed long-chassis Land
Rover borrowed from Ronnie's employer and carrying a
dozen bags of feed crumbs, an oil drum of barley and
another of water, along with an assortment of buckets
and tools. The sun was pleasantly shaded by high cloud
and there was a fitful but cooling breeze. I nursed the
vehicle over the lumpy track and parked it as close as I
could to the rock wall.

There was no way that I, or anybody else, could have
manhandled a filled oil drum to the upper level, but three
more empty drums with loose lids had been left beside

the gate to the pen. On the principle of getting the worst over first, I lugged bags of crumbs up the path, emptied them into the first drum and then filled the feeders. Mac wandered off for a look round.

Feeling in need of a rest, I did the required round of my uncle's snares, had a drink from my flask of tea, then set up the old semi-rotary pump and transferred the water from the drum on the Land Rover to the one at the upper level. To give myself another break I filled the waterers and set them out. I had brought with me two aerosols of paint and I set about painting huge eyes on the roofs of the two small shelters in the pen in the hope of frightening away the sparrowhawks. It seemed to me that if a butterfly can deter predators by simulating big eyes, the same might work for a pheasant pen.

Only the barley was left. It would be added to the crumbs in increasing proportions until they were feeding on barley alone. I began the slow business of filling two buckets at a time and carrying them up to fill the third drum. It was quicker and easier, I found, to step up on to the roof of the Land Rover's cab and from there on to the ground above the rock wall, and to return the same way.

I should have foreseen that during all this work it would be impossible to use both hands and still carry Ian's shotgun, so I had laid it at the edge of the rock wall with a brace of cartridges nearby, where I could grab them in one quick movement, either from the Land Rover or from the upper level. One of Dad's pistols in my pocket would have made more sense.

Or perhaps, as things turned out, it would only have got me killed.

When I turned round to see Mr Foster stepping from the roof of the Land Rover on to the ground ten feet from me, the shotgun was almost at his feet.

He stood with his back to the drop, neat as ever although he must have made a cautious approach across country. And just as polite.

'Good morning,' he said.

'We thought that you must be abroad by now,' was all that I could find to say.

He smiled thinly and I saw again the underlying coldness that I had seen before and which, I now realized, was part of the cruelty recognized by Mr Carmichael. 'And so I shall be before they find your body,' he said. 'I would have been in the Orient by now except that I had a score to settle.' He was holding Dad's Wildey .45 semi-auto pistol, but with a lack of familiarity which I found more unsettling than the pistol itself.

'A score? With me?' I asked innocently. He might be unaware of my part in his downfall.

'You've been in it all along,' he said judicially. 'But no. Even if you had never even heard of my existence, you would have been my target. You see, your father set the wheels in motion and your husband kept them rolling. Between them, they've wrecked my living and cost me a fortune. I knew that I couldn't get my hands on both of them. But there was one person whose death would hurt them both, worse than their own.' He smiled his chilly smile and a shiver ran up my back. 'You. Every time that your child misses its mother, they'll be reminded.' He watched me coldly, levelling the pistol, waiting for me to show fear.

My father, treating me always as an honorary boy, had taught me to stay calm in an emergency. A second's thought, he told me, was worth a minute's panic. But in that precious second I knew that panic might offer me my only chance. If the man wanted fear, I decided, he should have it. Perhaps, while it lasted, he would postpone the final act. So I did what I most wanted to do and screamed. There was even a chance that some stalker or hiker or forester might hear me . . .

The only voice to answer was the echo of my own, coming back seconds later from Crowborn Crag. There was another response, but not from a human being. Mac, who I had quite forgotten, tore out of the trees towards us. I saw that the hair was erect along his spine and his teeth were bared.

Foster shouted, 'Sit!' At the same moment, I cried, 'Kill!' I had no idea what commands the dog had been trained to, but the word seemed as good as any other.

Mac, with all of a dog's finely tuned senses, instantly recognized the menace which was fairly tainting the air around us. He crouched, growling deep in his throat. The spaniel in his makeup was submerged, the collie had come out on top – and a working collie can look the picture of menace. His eyes were on Mr Foster, a few feet away. It had taken him only an instant to decide between his former master and his new friend.

Foster was distracted from me. While his eyes and the pistol were turned away, I had my only chance. I threw myself forward. I seemed to move with ponderous slowness so that I had time for fear and thought. I intended at first to barge into him and hurl him over the rock wall. I would almost certainly go with him and we would both end up with broken bones, but I could see that if he was injured enough to make escape difficult, he would be mad to shoot me.

As I dived, the shotgun was under my nose. I grabbed it up by the barrels. It snapped shut of its own accord as I swung. Again I had time for a mind-change. I meant to swing at his head, but skulls are hard and I had enough guns to repair. As his hands came up, I switched in mid-swing and hit him as hard as ever I could in the midriff.

His breath came out in an explosive cough. He folded double and fell backwards off the rock wall.

If he had gone right to the ground he might have been crippled for life. If he had landed on the roof of the Land Rover he might have been unhurt and still able to shoot me. If he had fallen across one of the Land Rover's sides he would have broken his back. But he did none of these. Instead, quite by chance, he landed face-up in the open back of the Land Rover, in the drum which I had emptied of water. He was supported by the backs of his knees and the small of his back, but his elbow hit the edge of the oil drum and the pistol dropped out of his hand.

If he fought, he would soon free himself. I jumped down into the back of the Land Rover. The pistol had fetched up in the corner between the barrel and the side of the vehicle. I groped for it, found it and was standing up as he began to struggle. I had the pistol in my hand, safety off, and I was ready to shoot. But I straightened up under his feet and in raising them I deprived him of the support of his bent knees. He slipped further down until his armpits were taking his weight.

I said the first thing that came into my head. 'You shouldn't have killed Toby Douglas,' I told him. 'There wouldn't have been half the hue and cry if you hadn't. Why did you do it?'

His habitual politeness had vanished. The glare sat more naturally on his face than the smile had done. 'He had the bloody nerve to try and screw more money out of me.' Because of his cramped and doubled position, Foster's voice was strained. He made a sudden effort to pull himself up. It had not yet dawned on him that he had no leverage; and he thought of all women as victims.

'If you get out of there,' I said, 'you'll go back in upside-down and dead.'

He saw the pistol for the first time. 'Give me that,' he ground out and at the same time made a furious effort to escape from the grip of the barrel around his back and calves. It must have been a full half-minute before his energy burned itself out and he stopped, panting raucously and pouring sweat.

Another sound was getting through to me. I saw that Mac was down, his coat stained with blood, and it came back to me that I had heard the sound of a shot although at the time I had only been glad that it had not hit me. Taking the pistol with me, I stepped from the roof to the upper level and knelt down beside Mac. Foster's bullet had taken him through the spine and then, flattened and distorted, had exploded out through his underbelly. The finest veterinary surgeon in the world could not have saved him.

'I'm sorry, Mac,' I said. 'We could have got on. Bruce

would have loved you.' That is what I tried to say but the words would not quite come out. I took a look at my prisoner, but he was still firmly gripped. So I knelt down and stroked Mac's head and he licked my hand. When I judged that he had suffered enough and would be glad to be gone, I put my hand over his eyes, placed the muzzle of the pistol between his eye and his ear and shot him. It seemed the least that I could do for him and I hoped that somebody would have done as much for me. For a few seconds his front legs thrashed and his whole body trembled. Then he was still. Dad had been right, I thought. That pistol had a hell of a kick.

I stepped down into the back of the Land Rover. My vision was not as clear as usual and I nearly fell. Foster was struggling again in the barrel. I gave him a rap on the head with the pistol. He swore at me, a torrent of filth. I could ignore vile language when I wanted to, but I had no intention of taking it from Mac's killer. When I raised the pistol again, he put up his hands to avoid the blow . . . and slid the rest of the way into the barrel with only his feet showing and his arms from the elbows. He was, as I have said, a small man.

He said something. His voice was distorted by the reverberations in the barrel but I thought that he said something about a dog. 'The dog's dead,' I told him, 'and if you say another word, or if I see you make the least effort to get out of that barrel, I'll empty this pistol through the side of it.' I could hear the sound of my own voice and hardly recognized it. 'I'm going to dig a grave now. I can easily make it large enough for two.' And I think that I might have done it.

I was close to exhaustion after all the physical labour

of the day, but something drove me on. I collected the spade and dug a grave for Mac. I put him in it, said goodbye after my own fashion and filled it in.

The barrel was well secured. Mr Foster was croaking at me from deep in the barrel but I ignored him. If he cared to suffocate because of the pressure on his lungs, that was his affair. I took the driver's seat. My knees were shaking and I have never felt so tired. But I nursed the Land Rover along the track and then drove all the way into Newton Lauder, to park behind the Police HQ.

The sergeant on desk duty was an old friend. He drew himself up as I approached and said, 'Good afternoon, Mrs Fellowes.' He must have seen the blood on my clothes. If any other member of the public had walked in in such a state, there would have been a cell waiting within seconds, but I suppose that he assumed that I had been paunching rabbits or gralloching a deer.

'Would you call my husband?' I said. 'I have somebody outside who he very much wants to meet.'

Chapter Eleven

After all the hectic activity crammed into a mere three days, life seemed very slow but far from peaceful.

Ian, Bruce and I stayed on at Briesland House, partly so that, along with Dad as his recovery progressed, I could get on with preserving and restoring the antique guns but even more for the sake of security. Uncle Ronnie's employer, Sir Peter Hay, who was also my godfather, recalled a retired keeper to take over the duties and detached my uncle to act as bodyguard until any danger had gone by.

We were only too well aware that Mr Foster (as we continued to call him) was a man possessed by a demon of spite. He now had every cause to hate me in particular. Word was brought out of the prison where he was being held on remand that he had sworn terrible oaths, promising some fearsome revenge. As if that was not enough, there had also been anonymous calls, emanating from various phone-boxes and threatening death and worse if I gave evidence. Mr Foster himself might be behind bars but, Ian said, there were others with good cause to be apprehensive.

'Like who?' I demanded irritably. The combined forces of Dad, Ian and the police had restrained me from accepting an invitation to shoot at a prestigious estate near Kelso. My uncle, who was to have gone along as my loader, was equally indignant. I had had to admit that a day spent in the company of eight or ten armed individuals, several of them strangers, could hardly be considered to be 'keeping a low profile', but I had only agreed to pass up the once-in-a-lifetime invitation under protest. 'I can't see a jockey who's pulled up his horse having the motive or the clout to save Mr Foster's bacon.'

He looked at me as though I was dottled, perhaps with good cause. 'Politicians, for a start. Good God! Don't you read the papers?'

'Not very seriously,' I admitted. I go along with Dad's view. He holds that what comes out of Parliament is important, affecting as it does all our lives, but that what goes into Parliament, that is to say politicians, is as the dust under his feet. With very few exceptions, he says, politicians seem to consider that the prime reason for any decision will be whether or not it will enable them to retain or gain power at the next election. Fifty-five per cent of votes, he says, are cast with that objective in mind, forty per cent with a view to personal enrichment or advancement and the remainder with the intention of achieving what may be the best for the long-suffering electorate. He also says that the newspaper reports resemble reality as a child's crayon drawing of its mother resembles the lady in question.

'Well,' said my loving husband, 'if you tried to keep abreast of what's going on in the world, instead of confining your reading to the shooting and fishing magazines, you'd know that several different but very large scandals are brewing, with accusations flying around about the exchange of cash, and in one instance a peerage, for favours. There are some people with a lot of clout and a lot of motive for sweeping the whole thing under the carpet – and preferably somebody else's carpet.'

'I can't believe that anybody's biting his fingernails over what I might or might not say.'

'Why do you suppose the Eleventh Baron suddenly invited you to his family shoot?'

'I beat him at the trial for the British FITASC clay-pigeon team. He said at the time that he'd be interested to see what I could do at the grouse.'

'So he invites you to the pheasants,' Ian said. 'Be your age!' He considered me seriously for a few seconds, obviously wondering whether I was capable of coping with real grown-up discussion. (Some of Dad's attitude had rubbed off on him.) Evidently he decided that I was, because he went on, 'I've already been sounded out, so delicately that I almost didn't catch on at all, as to whether you would have a convenient memory lapse in exchange for a substantial sum of money.'

I was intrigued. 'What did you say?' I asked him.

'I said that you wouldn't.'

I dithered between being pleased by his faith in my integrity and furious that he should have made that particular answer on my behalf. If I was not to enjoy the possession of a pair of Purdeys and an Aston Martin, that should have been my decision and not his. I comforted myself with the thought that whoever had made the offer might have the same thought and try a more direct approach.

Despite Ian's arguments and my own experiences, I was only half convinced. But, just as a case against him

187

was reaching the point where an arrest was imminent, the unfortunate Mr Bentligger drowned in a swimming accident at Cramond although his few friends insisted that he had an acute dislike of cold water. And then the three toughs who had acted as Mr Foster's helpers and enforcers withdrew all previous statements but insisted on pleading guilty to everything that the Fiscal's office could throw at them, so that they disappeared inside with neither fuss nor publicity and threatening nobody. On the other hand, we heard that Mr Foster was saying nothing apart from a blanket denial of every charge against him.

So I kept Bruce close at hand, my uncle brooded over me like a mother hen and Ian watched over us all when he could and at other times saw to it that his colleagues were keeping an eye on us and on the environs of Briesland House.

Ian and I had written and sent to Tony McIver our formal statements about the case; but amplifying questions and answers were relayed through the Fiscal's office in Newton Lauder, so that I had been vaguely picturing the trial as taking place in the familiar and rather cosy local sheriff's courthouse. It was only when two formidably worded summonses were delivered by a uniformed inspector that it dawned on me that the murder had been committed in Grampian and the trial was to be in Aberdeen.

The day set for the trial approached, receded again as counsel and the advocate-depute manoeuvred around each other like dogs circling before a fight, and then approached once again as they ran out of excuses for further postponements. I packed a selection of my

soberer clothes and a dozen paperback novels I had
experienced the hours of waiting in dreary witness rooms
in the past.

The detailed arrangements had been in Ian's hands.
In my usual vague way I had envisaged, when I had
thought about it at all, a nervous journey by car carefully
limited to daylight and main roads, perhaps to stay with
Mr Munro again. But on a dreary February day a Range
Rover arrived at the door from Edinburgh, piloted by two
constables in plain clothes, each of whom I was sure was
armed. Near Perth, we pulled off the road to a small hotel
where we were transferred to a Jaguar from Aberdeen
after all four policemen, with Ian's active consent, had
enjoyed a pint, a good lunch and a chat.

We reached the Granite City as dusk was turning
into darkness. Later, I realized that the timing had been
deliberate. As the political scandal about graft and corruption had escalated, with both sides of the House and
several local authorities coming under public scrutiny,
the media had made the connection with the imminent
trial and were scouring Aberdeen for news, hints or rank
speculation. One glimpse of our arrival might soon have
come to the ears of others who might be watching and
waiting.

We were driven to a small Edwardian house of slate
and granite in a typical small tree-lined street midway
between the city centre and the sprawling outskirts and
we were delivered to a gate in a back lane. One of the
officers carried our bags for us, up a short garden path to
where a tall figure stood against the light in the doorway.
As my eyes adjusted I saw that this was Tony McIver. He

whisked us inside with no time for more than a quick
thank-you to our guardian angel.

Tony took our coats, led us through into a sitting room
where curtains were drawn over the windows and settled
us in fireside chairs. Inside, the house was not what
television had led me to expect of a 'safe house' provided
by the police. The furniture was modern and inexpensive
but comfortable. The colours chosen were youthful and
jolly. I had noticed brushes, pots and an electric stripper
tucked out of the way on the staircase. But there was a
real fire in the grate and bottles and glasses on a coffee
table. Somebody, it seemed, was anxious to please.

Tony was dressed simply in slacks, a polo neck and
a Walther PP Super 9 mm. semi-automatic in a holster
slung very professionally under his left armpit. With that
Highland lisp that so pleased my ear, he delivered a
speech of welcome which seemed to owe much of its
verve to the fact that he had emerged with credit from our
earlier collaboration. When he finished, I asked bluntly,
'Whose house is this?'

'Mine,' Tony said. He spoke with a touch of modest
pride, as well he might. For a young detective sergeant
to own even a small terrace house in oil-rich Aberdeen
was either an achievement or an invitation to the Personal Income Investigation Branch. 'Somebody has to
mother you, in case Mr Foster has the wrong sort of
friends. This seemed the safest and least conspicuous
way of doing it. I'm detached to act as your bodyguard
and driver until all this is over. In point of fact,' Tony
added, 'the accused's real name turns out to be Burk, but
it seems easier to go on calling him Foster.'

Ian nodded.

'Until all what is over?' I asked.

'Good question,' Tony said soberly. 'We don't know that you're in any danger but it seems safest to assume it. There have been some attempts to threaten witnesses. If the accused goes down the plug-hole, that should settle the matter. Nobody at liberty would have any reason to interfere with either of you.'

'And if he gets off?' I asked. I had a mental picture of Tony McIver following us around for ever.

'It's up to us to see that he doesn't,' Tony said. Then he brightened and was his usual cheerful self again. 'Meantime, I have the pleasure of looking after you here and the expenses claim that I'll put in will look like the national debt. If you get to see it, you'll be amazed how much you managed to eat and drink – starting now.' He became the eager young host to such good effect that I soon forgot to worry.

I was restive. I do not often manage to leave Bruce with my mother and spend a few nights in a city, within easy reach of theatres and other decadent delights. But no. My two guardians – for Ian had somehow managed to assume the dual roles of guardian and guardee – were adamant. Danger might not be lurking – but there was no profit in inviting trouble.

We spent that evening in front of Tony's television. In the morning, we made ourselves presentable for the High Court and then waited. We waited all day, playing Scrabble and muttering to ourselves. Periodically, Tony phoned the office of the Procurator Fiscal, but there had been no missed message. Counsel were arguing (some

191

might say quibbling) over procedural points before the judge. By the time the jury was in place, it was the end of the working day for lawyers.

Next day, by way of a change, Tony moved his car round to the lane and then hustled us out to it. The streets were full of traffic but nobody paid any attention to us. We pulled up at a side door of an old Gothic building on Union Street. Tony handed his car over to another man in plain clothes who seemed to have been waiting there for the purpose and, I was ready to guess, to chase away any suspicious lurkers, and the court policeman appeared and led the three of us in to a small but comfortable waiting room.

Another hour dribbled down the left leg of life while the constable who had been left to find the body told the court about the steps taken to secure the evidence. We ran out of conversation. I dug one of my novels out of Ian's briefcase, but my only interest in the question of who had murdered a professional footballer was a half-hearted hope that whoever had done it would get away with it.

Suddenly, Ian was called. As the arresting officer, he was to be the second witness. Tony stood in the waiting room doorway, his hand near the hidden holster, and watched Ian head for Number Six Court.

'Not long now,' he said. The words were well intentioned but they were all that was needed to set my stomach churning.

Ten long minutes later, the court policeman appeared suddenly in the doorway. I thought that he had come to call me, but he was frowning. 'Mrs Fellowes?' he said.

'There's a phone call for you. We wouldn't, usually, but he was very insistent. Come with me.'

Tony fell in on my heels. 'And hurry,' he said. 'Your husband's evidence can't last much longer.'

I was puzzled and slightly apprehensive. Had something happened to one of the family? The official led me over miles of red carpet, to a desk beside the entrance to a large atrium, where a phone lay beside its rest. I picked it up and said, 'Yes?'

A rough voice, with an accent which I thought of as being from Edinburgh, seemed to speak right in my ear. 'We've got your little boy, Mrs F.,' it said. 'If you give your evidence or if you tell the court about this call, he's dead and you'll never know were he's buried.' In the second before he disconnected, I could hear a baby crying in the background.

Tony said later that he saw my colour vanish as though a lamp had been switched off. I thought that I was going to faint, yet my mind was still functioning. I got the dialling tone and keyed the code for Newton Lauder. The macer said, 'Here!' and reached for the phone, but I struck his hand aside. Tony, who must have guessed the general nature of events, pulled him back. Tony also had the sense not to interrupt me with unanswerable questions.

In the distance, a voice was calling for *Mrs Deborah Fellowes*, but it had nothing to do with me.

At Briesland House, the phone still rang. I kept telling myself that that had not been Bruce's voice, that it had been the crying of a younger baby. I told myself that if anything had happened to Bruce I would have been told, but I knew that they would probably have kept any such news from me.

'You'd better tell me,' Tony said. 'Then we must go.'

I shook my head at him. Rather than argue, he put his ear next to mine.

Had my fumbling fingers misdialled while trying at the same time to hold on to my sanity? I was on the point of cancelling the call and trying again when there was a click at the far end and Dad's voice came on the line. He sounded breathless.

'Is Bruce all right?' I cried.

I must have sounded quite unlike my usually tranquil self, because he said, 'Who is this?'

'It's me, Deborah. Is—?'

'He's all right, Toots,' Dad said. 'But there was a man walked in on us about twenty minutes ago, carrying a shotgun. He seemed to think that that made him top dog. He should have known that this family is probably a damn sight more familiar with guns than he is. Your mother hit him with a frying pan full of hot fat, I took the gun off him and Ronnie, not to be left out of things, pulled him like a wishbone.'

For some reason, in my great relief the words *frying pan* caught my ear. 'Mum isn't giving Bruce fried food, is she?'

'No, no. She—'

Tony terminated the call by putting his finger on the button. 'If you don't want to be held in contempt of court,' he said, 'go, go, go.'

The official, who seemed to be in full agreement with Tony's view, caught hold of my wrist and pulled me almost running on shaking legs across more red carpet until, quite suddenly, I was in the courtroom and tripping over the step up into the witness box. I found myself facing the jury in their playpen, with a field of pink faces in the fully occupied public seats to one side of me and a judge in wig and robes glaring down at me from a great height on the other. But I was more aware of Mr Foster, in the dock, emitting waves of hatred.

I became aware that the judge was addressing me in tones of reproof. He finished with a sharp question. I pulled my scattered wits together. 'My Lord,' I said, 'I received a threatening message that my baby son had been kidnapped and that his life would be in danger if I gave evidence. I took time to phone home. There had been an attempt at kidnapping but it had failed.'

There was a quick buzz, as quickly silenced by the judge. There was scribbling in notebooks from where I supposed the reporters were sitting. I was beginning to calm down and, looking beyond the wig and robes, I saw that he had a mild though jowly face and that he was raised only a very few feet above the level of the rest of the room.

I was left to sit and stare blankly at the painted panels for several minutes while the judge issued some stern instructions which I was too dazed to take in. A handwritten note was laid before him and he nodded and looked down at me.

'Mrs Fellowes,' he said, 'do you feel able to give evidence now, without fear or favour?'

I said that I did. And I took the oath.

At last, the advocate-depute rose to take me through my evidence. Guided by his questions, I spoke of my early suspicions as to Mr Foster's bona fides and continued through the whole story, finishing with the attack on me at the release pen. While I spoke, Foster never removed his cold eyes from my face except to scribble an occasional note for his counsel.

When my testimony finished, His Lordship glanced at the clock and decided that the court would adjourn for lunch. My cross-examination could wait until court resumed. It seemed that the precautionary measures were not yet over, because I was led back to the same witness room, where Tony was waiting for me with a cold lunch on a tray.

'What about yourself?' I asked him.

'I have a date for lunch with your husband when you go back in the witness box.'

I was disappointed but hardly surprised. My vision – of being taken out for a sustaining lunch full of cholesterol and all that is a threat to long life – faded. But at least Tony or somebody had managed to provide me with a miniature bottle of a rather nasty red wine. Before reluctantly taking a bite out of a cold pork pie I asked Tony to tell me what had developed while I waited in the witness box.

He nodded and poured my wine into a plastic imitation wineglass. 'I heard some of what you were told on the phone,' he said, 'and I could guess most of the rest. It seemed obvious that they'd tried to time it for just before you were called. That would make sense. No time left for countermeasures and if you'd had the required attack of amnesia they could have returned your son immediately without even having to change a nappy.

'But that sort of timing required somebody here to observe the progress of the trial and pass the word along when the optimum moment was approaching. Presumably he would have stayed on to report as soon as you had committed yourself. But you walked into the court and told His Lordship about the threat. He would certainly need to pass that information along. Even if he had a mobile phone, he wouldn't be allowed to use it in the court-room. So I dashed to the exit used by the public and waited to see who came out.

'A few seconds later a man ducked out and headed for the public phones. Then he changed his mind and made for the street. If he was the observer, I didn't want to lose him. So I took him aside and invited him to answer a few questions. He was mightily indignant and since he was also well dressed and well spoken I might easily have fallen for it, but one of the officers on duty had had a similar thought and followed the sound of angry voices. He recognized my friend as a former embezzler turned fixer. The gentleman is now being interrogated at HQ and with a little luck we'll soon know the identities of not only the gang but their client as well.'

I pushed aside the remains of a cheese sandwich. 'In that case,' I said, 'the danger is past and you've covered yourself in glory once again. What's more, we still have time for you to take me out for a lovely, fattening lunch.'

'I'm afraid not,' Tony said sympathetically. 'Literally dozens of influential and well-heeled people may have motives for wanting Foster released and spirited abroad. And pressure could still be put on you to blow up under cross-examination. As it is, you may get a rather rough ride. Better prepare yourself to stay calm and to remember that Foster's advocate is only doing a job. He's being very well paid to present his client in as good a light as he possibly can. There's nothing personal in it. And he can't bite you – at least, I've never known it to happen.'

I unwrapped a small and ice-cold apple pie. 'I'd hate to form a precedent. Perhaps he'd like to bite this instead? Or perhaps you would?'

Tony studied the soggy pastry and tried not to pull a face. 'I don't want to spoil my lunch,' he said.

The moment which I had been dreading arrived. Foster's advocate rose to cross-examine me.

The going seemed easy. He led me through my earlier evidence, asking me whether I was sure, whether there was no room for doubt or how I could be certain of the details. To conquer my nerves I tried to imagine him without the wig. My memory was jogged when he addressed me as 'Miss Calder'.

'I understood the witness to be Mrs Fellowes,' the judge put in.

'I beg your pardon, my lord, and that of Mrs Fellowes. I did not intend to return her to the single state. Mrs Fellowes, I had forgotten that you had married . . . a policeman?' Counsel did not sound abashed and I began to wonder how much he knew.

I admitted having married into the police. At the same time, recognition came rushing at me. I could see him a little younger and much less confident, at the Pentland Gun Club during the brief period when I had stood in as secretary and principal coach. His name was Roberts or Robertson, something like that. I began to relax a little. He had been sold a gun which fitted him badly and bruised him, as a result of which he was flinching and missing nine 'birds' out of ten. I had taken him in hand, made a temporary and then a permanent alteration to his gun and then given him a little coaching. He had been a rewarding pupil and when he had begun to wipe the floor with the legal cronies who had been laughing at his earlier failure he was pathetically grateful.

But gratitude, it seemed, had no place in our present dialogue.

'Married to a policeman,' he said, almost musingly. 'In fact, your husband has already given evidence as the arresting officer. And here you are, giving evidence for the police. I withdraw the comment,' he added quickly before the judge could pull him up. 'Mrs Fellowes, do you regard yourself as a truthful person?'

'Certainly,' I said.

'Indeed? I am not referring to those little white lies that all of us tell from time to time. You are not given to telling what are known as "whoppers"?' There was a whisper of amusement in the courtroom.

I said that I was not.

'Nor to condone lies told by others?'

I could only say 'no', but something nasty was coming.

'Mrs Fellowes, according to your testimony neither you nor your companions saw a body at the former farmhouse known as Mowdiemoss.'

I felt myself go white and then flush. Mr Foster was giving me the look that I had seen on his face when he confronted me at the release pen. Among the other faces, Ian's seemed to stand out. There was no comfort for me there. What had he got hold of and how the devil had he got it?

'Well? Answer the question, Mrs Fellowes.'

I pulled myself together. Perhaps the manageress at the tearoom had overheard, or gossip had leaked from among the police. That no longer mattered. 'I don't think that I said quite that,' I told him.

'Perhaps not. Shall we check? I took down your words, but if you doubt my accuracy the court reporter can read it back to us.'

'Let's hear your version,' I said. 'I'll soon tell you if you've got it wrong.'

'I expect you will.' There was already several markers in the large notebook in front of him and he opened the book with a triumphant rustle. 'These, I think, were your words. "The dog led me to Mowdiemoss farmhouse, where the body was later discovered." Well, Mrs Fellowes?'

'That sounds about right.'

'One of your husband's colleagues, a Constable' – he flipped to another marker – 'Constable Murchieson, testified to finding the body after you, your husband and another officer had left the scene. But is it not true that the body was seen by at least one of your party before you made your departure? Please remember that you are on oath.'

I took a deep breath. Supporting a fib from one policeman to another was one thing. Committing perjury would be quite another. If I evaded a direct response by some such answer as *I believe so*, I would soon be pinned down and, in the process, my own sighting of the body might emerge. I found that my mouth had gone dry.

'Yes,' I said. And the fat was in the fire.

'And no doubt you would argue that the statement

you made to the court earlier was literally true. But
would you not agree that it was, to say the least, mislead-
ing?' While I was still struggling to find the right words,
he went on, 'And is it not true that your husband and his
colleague, with your connivance, allowed – I will not put
it stronger than this – allowed a senior officer to believe
that you had all three left the scene without suspecting
that a dead body lay in one of the outbuildings?'

'The way it was—' I began.

'Surely the question is susceptible of a yes or no
answer.'

I looked at the advocate-depute, hoping that he might
find some technical objection to this line of questioning.
He met my eye but looked away again.

'Yes,' I said.

'And you still consider yourself to be a truthful
person?'

The judge leaned forward. 'An unanswerable question, Mr Robson,' he said. 'I think that you've made your
point. Shall we move on?'

I called down blessings on his bewigged head and
silently promised his gun a free overhaul if he should
care to bring it to us.

Counsel sketched a bow to the judge. 'Mrs Fellowes,'
he said, 'now that we have a measure of your regard for
the truth, let us take another look at the evidence you
have given.'

And another look we did indeed take. But, this time
around, my degree of certainty was put under the micro-
scope. I had become suspicious of the accused because
of his estate car? How could I be certain that he had not
bought the car in good faith? Had I seen the accused at

the scene of the robbery? Had I seen any of my father's property at Mowdiemoss? Had I seen the accused at Bonnypark?

I struggled to make my answers as firm and clear as I could. Sometimes I was forced to modify what I had previously said and then counsel would glance significantly at the jury. The court was quiet and the only distracting movement in my peripheral vision was of the pencils of two reporters at the front of the public seats. Several times the advocate-depute objected that questions had already been asked and answered but he was overruled.

At last we returned to the subject of the final confrontation. Here at least, I thought, I was on firm ground. But having impressed the court with my unreliability and untruthfulness as a witness, counsel went in for the kill.

'When the accused managed to find you at last, why were you so sure that his intentions were hostile?'

'He was holding a firearm that had earlier been stolen from my father,' I said, 'and pointing—'

'It didn't occur to you that he might be seeking to return some property which had fallen into his hands?'

'No. For one thing, the pistol was loaded.'

He clicked his tongue. I remembered him making the same noise when a clay pigeon got past him on the driven grouse stand. 'Even if my client, who does not have your experience with firearms, had been rash enough to bring the pistol to you in a loaded state, you did not know that until later. Did you?'

'No,' I admitted. 'But I was entitled to infer it from—'

'You inferred it and on the basis of that inference you

assaulted him brutally with a shotgun. Did you ask him whether the pistol was loaded?'

If he was going to persist in cutting me off before I had finished my answer, I decided to make sure that the punchline came first. 'He was telling me that he was going to kill me,' I said. 'It hardly seemed to be a necessary question.'

'Ah yes,' he said, as though pleased that I had reminded him. 'This alleged threat. It did not occur to you that, approaching you as he was with a pistol in his hands, he might possibly have tried to alleviate any possible tension by making a jocular remark?'

'No it did not. Guns and humour do not go together.'

'Do they not? I seem to recall occasions at the Pentland Gun Club when considerable humour was bandied about.'

I wondered whether to remind him that the humour had often been at his expense, but decided that he would undoubtedly turn the thrust against me. 'There may have been some teasing,' I said, 'but handling a deadly weapon is not intrinsically funny.'

'Is that so? Was there never an occasion when you were standing with a loaded gun in your hands and you called out to a beater to come out with his hands up?'

'That was my uncle,' I protested. 'It was quite different. I was joking,' I added on a fatal impulse.

The court-room stirred. I saw the advocate-depute close his eyes in pain. But my tormentor decided to leave well alone. 'Mrs Fellowes,' he said, 'I suggest that you have exaggerated a piece of horseplay by somebody you disliked and mistrusted into an excuse to assault him.'

'No,' I said hoarsely.

'I further suggest that you have continued to exaggerate and distort your evidence in order to please your very good friends in the police force.' His tone of voice suggested that I was the mistress of half the constabulary. And with that he sat down.

The advocate-depute rose, to repair the damage if he could. He held a note in his hand which I assumed was from Ian or Tony. 'Mrs Fellowes, you told the court, quite truthfully, that you arrived at Mowdiemoss farmhouse, where the body of the victim was later found. The court had already heard Constable Murchieson testify to finding the body. But you have now told my friend that you and your companions saw the body before Constable Murchieson's arrival.'

'May I explain?' I asked.

'I was about to invite you to do so.'

I took a deep breath. 'I had no intention of deceiving the court on any point of importance. We arrived at Mowdiemoss. We had heard the sound of a vehicle and there was a lingering smell of fuel in the air. We did see the body. It seemed to have been dead for only a very short time. So it seemed certain that the murderer was still in the act of fleeing. There was one witness nearby who could give us a vital clue as to where the murderer might be headed. But only one member of our party was an officer with Grampian Police and if he reported finding the body, routine would keep him tied up for ages and there would be delay before that witness could be interviewed. We held an urgent discussion and decided to let Constable Murchieson make the discovery – officially.

After that, it became difficult to . . to tell it any other way.'

'I understand. Thank you.' The advocate-depute sat down.

A few minutes later, court was adjourned.

Chapter Twelve

Before I left the court-room the advocate-depute caught
me. He was not looking pleased but he avoided rebuk-
ing me. He had removed his wig and looked quite human,
more like a farmer than a senior advocate. 'Come back
tomorrow morning,' he said. 'You may be needed again.'

'So that the judge can give me a slap on the wrist?'

'Oh, I don't think it'll come to that.' He gave me an
encouraging pat on the shoulder and hurried off. I followed in his wake, cursing my luck. I had been hoping
to finish my evidence and to have been on the road home
that evening.

Tony and Ian were waiting at the door, each looking
as guilty as sin itself. 'Well, what was I supposed to do?' I
asked defensively before recriminations could start flying
around. 'Commit perjury? How do you suppose he found
out about it? One of your mob,' I told Tony severely, 'must
have shot his mouth off.'

'Possibly,' Tony said. 'That'll be looked into.' He
glanced around. Nobody was within earshot but I was
getting curious looks from one or two of the dispersing
public further off. 'This isn't the place to talk about it. I
know a pub near here that stays open in the afternoons.
Come on.'

We sneaked out by the same side door. The pub was almost empty at that time and Tony settled us in a quiet corner where the omnipresent musak would smother our voices. He fetched beer for himself and Ian but I felt the need of a brandy. He bought me a large one and a ginger ale without complaining.

'You'll have the Police Association down on your neck,' Ian told him, 'if you start a witch-hunt for the one who dropped you in the clag.'

Tony shook his head. 'Nobody dropped me in anything. I'd already had my dressing down from Mr Goth, and very mild he was about it. I think he could see that it was an honest attempt to bend the rules in the right direction. The man I'm going to hunt,' he said grimly, 'is the swine who blew a hole through the middle of a strong prosecution case, to get back at me or, more likely, to earn himself a fistful of notes. I admit that I'm worried.'

'Never mind,' Ian said. 'Foster will still get sent down. Won't he?'

'I wish I could be sure of it.' Tony sighed. 'Witnesses have been dropping out like . . . like soup through a colander. Bribed or intimidated or both. Even Willy Paterson's overweight girlfriend suddenly can't remember whether Foster was the man who used to come to the caravan. And now our misdeed is out in the daylight. You did your best to repair it – and a good best it was,' he told me kindly, 'but your evidence will probably be discounted. And they've given notice of a defence of alibi.'

'Surely,' I said, 'the kind of witnesses he could command—'

'Don't you believe it!' Tony snorted. 'The upper

echelons of the criminal fraternity command a lot of money and carry a lot of clout.'

This was a new and very unwelcome line of thought. Until then, I had been secure in the knowledge that Mr Foster was going up the river for a long, long time.

'If he walks free . . .' Ian said. He glanced at me.

'That,' said Tony, 'is why I'm worried. We can start by following him. You can guard Mrs Fellowes. You know as well as I do that neither of us can do so indefinitely. But Foster could wait a lifetime for his opportunity. That is if he really carries a grudge and means to pay it off, which would be in line with his reputation – and his performance so far. We shall have to do some serious thinking. In the meantime, do we feel like painting the town?'

'I suppose it's safe,' said Ian.

Tony looked at him pityingly, Inspector or not. Sometimes I thought that young Tony was getting a bit above himself. 'Of course it's safe,' he said. 'She's given her evidence and been cross-examined. Nobody has anything to gain by harming her now. If she withdrew her evidence tomorrow it wouldn't make a whole lot of difference, in view of all the doubt that's been thrown at it. Only maniacs like Foster take violent action when there's nothing to be gained.'

I was in thorough agreement. But I had presented myself in court with the appearance of a thoroughly trustworthy middle-class housewife. I had put a posh frock into my case, in anticipation of persuading Ian into a night out. But, 'I'll have to get my hair done,' I told them.

The two men exchanged a quick look, both nodded

and Tony gave me directions to a salon not very far off. 'We'll wait here,' Ian said.

'I bet you will,' I told them. But if they wanted to discuss how best to protect me without subjecting me to the worry of listening to them, let them. It gave me a cosy feeling of being pampered.

The salon was busy but they managed to fit me in. I had the full treatment and was back at the pub, now filling with the evening trade, within a couple of hours. They were at the same table with, as far as I could see, the same two empty pint glasses in front of them.

'Who is this gorgeous lady who is accosting us?' Tony cried, with what I thought was forced jollity.

Ian retorted in kind. 'That's no lady, that's my old woman. Good God! How much did that cost?' he demanded, coming down to earth.

'I don't know,' I said. 'I used Access.'

They could not have been sitting at the table the whole time, because they had managed, so they told me, to phone and book a table at a good restaurant and stalls at His Majesty's Theatre.

'I vote in favour,' I said. 'But is it safe?'

'Good God!' Ian said. 'Even if he knew where to look for you, he wouldn't recognize the new you.'

Despite my long absence, we still had time to return to Tony's house and pretty ourselves.

As promised, we painted the town. We went from the restaurant to the theatre to a nightclub and finished up doing a little modest gambling. An added touch of luxury was that Tony insisted on the use of taxis. Although we were usually very careful at home, I was in no doubt that, provided nobody was driving dangerously, Ian's in-laws were considered to be beyond the reach of the breathalyzer.

I had dreaded seeing what the morning papers had made of what I regarded as my total humiliation, but in fact the story was shunted off the front pages and dwarfed by a report, attributed to a 'reliable source', that Mr Foster was preparing to do a deal with the authorities and had already signed a contract to sell his story for 'a six-figure sum' to one of the national dailies. Several persons in positions of authority had hastened to deny that any deal was in the wind or even permissible, for what that was worth.

My own first reaction was one of relief. If Mr Foster was wiping the slate clean and starting afresh in the full light of day and with money in the bank, he would surely be less likely to pursue vengeance for past injuries.

I got through two of my paperbacks that day, sitting alone in the small witness room while various prosecution witnesses failed to live up to their precognitions. Late in the afternoon, the advocate-depute came to tell me that my usefulness was almost certainly over, but would I please attend in the morning, just in case?

Tony had other fish to fry that evening, so Ian and I borrowed his car and drove out to visit Mr Munro and his sister. The ex-Chief Superintendent, who had been following the case as reported in the media, was properly indignant at the failure of the justice system. He was full of sympathy over my rough handling under cross-examination and I thought that I could detect a trace of guilt, like a small boy caught stealing apples, that by allowing himself to be seduced away from the rule-book he had contributed to my downfall.

Now that I was out of danger, we had offered to move to a hotel, but Tony would not hear of it. So we all met over the breakfast table next morning when the big news broke.

Mr Foster had been found hanged in his cell.

A telephoned query through the office of the Procurator Fiscal confirmed the obvious, that my presence would no longer be required, so after one last good breakfast Tony drove us to the railway station. There were no vacant parking spaces, so we said our thanks and farewells in the forecourt and saw him drive off.

We caught an Edinburgh InterCity with a few minutes to spare. Once we were under way, I staggered along the swaying corridor to the payphone near the buffet car and phoned home. Dad, who had caught the news on the radio and had expected the call, promised to collect us from Edinburgh Waverley.

I settled back opposite Ian. The train was almost empty and none of the seats at our end of the coach was occupied. 'Now,' I said, 'you can tell me what really happened.'

He tried not to show any reaction but I have learned to read him like a book. His eyes seemed to meet mine but they were focused on a point high on my forehead. 'You know as much as I do,' he said. He pretended to go back to his *Scotsman*. I thought of setting fire to the paper but I would have had to ask him for the match. In the end, I found that speaking to the back of the paper was almost as effective.

'At first,' I said, 'I believed what I was being told. But all day yesterday, when you could have relaxed because there was no threat for the moment, you two were like cats on hot bricks. This morning, you had both relaxed.'

Ian put down the paper and looked at me indignantly. 'It never occurred to you that it might be because the threat to you was now permanently over?'

'It occurred to me, yes. But with Mr Foster now in the past, all the work that everybody did to get so close to breaking up the gang, it's all gone down the pan. Hasn't it?'

'As a matter of fact, Clever-clogs, it hasn't,' Ian said, descending to the language of the schoolroom. I thought for a moment that he was going to put his tongue out at me. Instead, he looked round to be quite sure that we were alone. 'Word has been filtering through from Edinburgh. Mr Bentligger kept his correspondence and records on a computer. He wiped his files off the hard disc and thought that they had gone for ever. That was the story that went round. But they were still in there somewhere and an expert has been able to recover them. Some of the names you wouldn't believe,' Ian added with satisfaction.

'So Mr Foster couldn't have done a deal anyway,' I suggested.

'Exactly.'

'Aha!' I said, so sharply that this time he really did jump. 'I thought so. All that guff about deals and selling his autobiography to the papers was pure fiction. I suppose you cooked it up while I was at the hairdresser?'

Ian wondered whether to try to bluff it out, but he could see that I was not going to let go until I had the truth. He changed his mind so suddenly that he was still shaking his head when he began to speak. 'Not pure,' he said. 'Far from it. Believe me, we did a whole lot of heart-searching before we set it up.'

'I bet. Who actually went in and hung him up?'

Ian looked at me in horror. 'Nobody! At least, nobody we'd know. You mustn't think that. All that we did was plant the story. Tony phoned a friend who acts as a stringer for two of the national dailies. After that, the matter looked after itself. As Tony told us, the upper echelons of the criminal fraternity have a lot of money and a hell of a lot of clout. I think that those were his words, near enough. Well, the establishment has a damn sight more money and all the clout in the world.'

'The establishment?'

Ian shrugged. 'I can't give you all the facts. No doubt they're only now emerging from Mr Bentligger's RAM disc. But do you not remember that, not long after an arms deal with General Hanrami's government was announced, a minister opened up the boxes containing his grandfather's book collection and found first editions and folios worth hundreds of thousands? And a hitherto unknown painting by Turner was discovered just after orders for new frigates were placed with foreign ship-yards?'

There was silence between us until we had passed Stonehaven. 'Well, I think it was absolutely immoral,' I said at last. 'The two of you planted a story that set him up to be murdered. That's what we're saying, isn't it?'

'I invite you to remember two things,' Ian said coldly.

'Firstly, the man had already committed a murder and looked set to get away with it. And, secondly, we were both concerned for you. If he had walked free, your life might not have been worth much.'

'All the same,' I said more mildly, 'you must admit that a little thing like not reporting a dead body fades into insignificance by comparison. What do you think Mr Goth would say if he knew?'

Ian raised his eyebrows before picking up the paper. 'Tony cleared it with Mr Goth before we did anything else,' he said.

Back at Briesland House, once Bruce had got over the shock of seeing me with a new hairdo, Mum and I settled for a chat over a cup of tea.

'Would you promise me something?' she asked me.

'Of course,' I said, wondering what I was letting myself in for.

'Try to stop your father getting into any more excitements.'

'Me?'

'You have more influence with him than anyone else,' she said, surprising me. 'This isn't the first time he's landed in hospital. Over the years, I don't know how often he's got us involved in things. Did you know that I was stabbed once, before you were born? Another time, you were kidnapped to put pressure on him. And now, just when I thought he'd grown out of all that nonsense, we have threats to my only grandchild and I bent my best frying pan and I still haven't got all the fat off the floor and it's getting too much.'

I felt a surge of remorse. When I came to think of it, Mum had often borne the brunt when Dad and I had been haring off on some mad chase. 'But I don't see what I can do,' I said.

Mum put down her cup. I heard it jingle in the saucer. She really was upset. 'If you think back,' she said, 'I bet there was a moment when you could have stopped him getting involved. Wasn't there?'

I thought back to our early talks and in particular to Kenneth Foggarty's visit. Perhaps she was right. 'I'll see what I can do,' I said.

There is little left to say that is worth saying. The scandal, the attempted cover-up and the wholesale prosecutions that followed must be part of history by now.

The death of Mr Foster, apparently by his own hand, made it impossible to comply with the strict terms of the insurance company's reward offer. The argument rumbles on and a settlement remains a distant prospect. But then, I suppose that insurance companies must get so used to being ripped off that they come to consider ripping off to be a normal business practice.

Author's Note

As far as I am aware, neither the Standard Supervisory Department nor the Personal Income Investigation Branch exist. They should do but they don't.

So relax!

GH